A Wild Justice

By the same author

HONOUR THE SHRINE
THE TREMBLING EARTH
OVERDUE
SOMETHING TO LOVE
ACT OF MERCY
A BATTLE IS FOUGHT TO BE WON
TIME IS AN AMBUSH
THE GREEN FIELDS OF EDEN
THE HUNTING-GROUND
THE THIRD SIDE OF THE COIN
THE NAKED RUNNER
ALL MEN ARE LONELY NOW
ANOTHER WAY OF DYING
THE BLIND SIDE

FRANCIS CLIFFORD

A Wild Justice

HODDER AND STOUGHTON
LONDON SYDNEY AUCKLAND TORONTO

475015559

ORMSKIRK

For Dodo and Mark

I

The moment the man emerged into the open spaces of the Green she saw him in the broken piece of mirror angled slightly above her head, and she reached for the rifle.

All the leaves were down. The shattered bandstand and the leprous skeletons of a few trees were the man's only cover, yet he walked upright and at even pace, as if convinced that the tide of danger had reached for good to other areas of the city. With a kind of disbelief she watched him stride diagonally across the near corner of the Green—an officer, revolver holstered outside his greatcoat, coming nearer at every step.

She raised herself cautiously over the heap of rubble and poked the rifle forward, releasing the safety-catch, deaf to everything except the rising hammer-hammer of her heart.

A captain, narrow face, fair moustache; he was that close already, the greatcoat flapping around his knees.

She hunched her right shoulder and fixed him with hazel-brown eyes, nestled her cheek against the small of the butt and pinned him silently in the centre of his chest with the foresight.

Time seemed to hover. Gently she took first pressure on the trigger, squeezing, every muscle in her body taut, every part of her mind empty of feeling, breath held, the whole of her life and being narrowed into the intensity of each standstill second.

Now, she thought.

A tree-trunk hid the captain between paces. She delayed fractionally, slewing a shade from right to left, nailing him again. Then suddenly a hand was clamped across her eyes and another wrenched the rifle away. The hands came from behind and, simultaneously, a voice breathed furiously in her ear:

"Jesus, girl, have you taken leave of your senses?"

She whimpered, blinded, hearing the footsteps pass. Raging, she clawed the hand from her face and twisted round.

"I had him!"

"Any fool—"

"I had him, for sure!"

"Listen—"

"Let go of my arm!"

"Idiot. *Idiot*, you."

All this in whispers, spat back and forth, frosting on the air. The girl's glance scattered away across the Green but the officer had disappeared. She turned her head again, glaring.

"Give me the gun."

"Not to an idiot, I won't."

"The gun," she demanded. "Let me have it."

"There's Kenny and me with lives to lose besides yours. Go somewhere else if it's suicide you're set on."

"He was a dead man."

"I tell you, Clodagh, they won't leave a mouse living if they bring up an armoured car. And they will if you give this position away. They'll blast us to the sky."

Her eyes leaked with the cold. She pressed against the rubble, resentment injected into the low fierce voice. "What's the point of being here?"

No answer.

"I'm asking you," she insisted. "What's the point of being here if all we're going to do is watch the bastards strut this way and that in front of our noses?"

"We're to wait."

"Wait's become a litany of a word."

"Not only for you."

"Liam's right," the one called Kenny muttered weakly, "and you know it. Don't start on that again."

"We'll starve if we wait much longer."

"Not for a day or so," Liam said.

Clodagh Lacey jerked her head. "Holy Mother."

"There'll be a counter-attack before then. And until there is we lie quiet. Didn't we agree on it? Sure it's galling to hold yourself in. Patience never comes easy when one of their kind's in sight." Liam snapped the safety-catch down and passed the rifle back to the girl. "You'll have chances enough yet. Save yourself for what they bring."

They were one floor up, in what remained of a bathroom in what had once been a small commercial hotel. Shellfire had destroyed almost the entire front of the building and the smashed joists protruded at each level like broken ribs. Some of the inner walls had gone, too, but the bathroom was still enclosed on three sides and shielded on the fourth by a waist-high mound of broken brick and mortar.

Liam had chosen the place. The fighting had been fiercest around the Green and devastation was everywhere. He could have found a score of holes for them to hide in, but the need for water had weighed with him even when panic jabbered that cover alone was enough. It was night then, the clouds glowing like coals as flames licked the sky, the buildings like ghosts of their former selves.

"Here," he had yelled above the crackling din. "Over here," and Clodagh and Kenny had heard and stumbled in his wake. Now water dripped from a brass tap into a plaster-choked bath and it was day, the second belly-empty day, afternoon, and the fighting sounded spasmodically in the near distance like twigs snapping.

Liam Gallagher was thirty-five. Beneath the beard-stubble his face was the colour of used candle-grease. When he smiled he held the smile tight so as not to expose bad blackened teeth, but he had almost forgotten how; smiles and laughter belonged to the past. The fingers of his right hand were stained with nicotine darker than his hair and his nails were broken and filthy. It was a week since he had shaved, five days since he'd gathered with others in a cobbled yard and been given a gun and general absolution, forty-eight hours since he'd eaten. He was wearing brown boots which were split across the insteps, stained black trousers, a collarless shirt and a baggy tweed jacket gone bald at the elbows. On his head he had a grey cloth cap turned back to front so that the peak flattened over his neck.

And he was cold, raw cold, deep into the bones.

They all were, though Clodagh showed it least. She had alarmed him just now, but in some respects he marvelled at her. She was tough and agile and could shoot like a marksman. When they issued the rifles in the yard and they were being grouped into squads of three or four he had thought in the shuffling darkness that she was a boy. Her hair was short enough and she was dressed like one, with an old army tunic buttoned to the throat.

"Have you got your ammo?"

"Twelve clips."

Dismayed, he'd peered close. "You're a woman, aren't you? God Almighty, so you are—you're a woman."

"What's that to you?"

She was never less than defiant, never anything but brave. But there was a wildness in her, a lack of discipline. Five days after surviving together, and beginning grudgingly to marvel, he thought sometimes that she was possessed of a fiery simplicity, an innocence almost, and when he decided this was what he detected in her he was scared. All things truly terrible stemmed from innocence, and hers could be the death of them yet.

He winced when he considered how close she had come to killing the officer and the retaliation that would surely have followed. The stillness that had settled over the Green was a deception: a look-out post was at the southern end, close to a gutted tram, and less than an hour earlier a Whippet armoured car had nosed into the adjacent side street.

"Take it easy," he said as a postscript. "Calm yourself, girl."

She had neat, sharp-looking teeth in very pale gums. Her lips were also pale, her cheeks concave, her skin white and smooth over the bones, her cropped hair reddish-gold.

13

"Where did you learn to handle a gun?"

"At home."

"Where's home?"

"Where I'm from."

Only a few feet ever separated them and their voices scarcely rose above a whisper.

"Who cut your hair like that?"

"They did."

"When?"

"When they killed my father."

Everyone who took up arms nursed a terrible grief, or a resentment, or an idea. A memory of his own twisted in Liam like a knife and suddenly he was unable to distract himself from the cold any longer; it seemed to shrink his insides. He shivered, listening to the slow soggy dripping from the tap, then shifted position and reached for the piece of mirror wedged on the lip of the rubble, moving it from side to side so as to observe the Green and the ruined buildings that squared it in. The tops were gone from some of them; all were streaked and stained, the window-sockets blind.

When he was a child his parents used to bring him to the Green on a summer's Sunday afternoon to listen to the band. Before the century turned, this was, with one world all but dead and the other powerless to be born. "Gorgeous," they would say, indicating the mellow Georgian façades. "Aren't they gorgeous, Liam?"

It wasn't beauty he looked for now. He swivelled the glass so that he could concentrate on the area by the tram-car. Nothing stirred, no one moved, but they were there—above the burned-out baker's shop. He knew it. And not only there. Closer than that. Somewhere to the left of them, out of sight, around the Green's near corner, wherever the captain had been heading.

Sodding bastards.

Kenny Doyle's teeth chattered and Liam started; his nerves flinched at the least unheralded sound. He gazed at Kenny's gaunt, pock-marked face and found himself unexpectedly capable of pity. Kenny was thin and wasted and gangling, approaching thirty. Bare-headed, he had on a fawn overcoat several sizes too large which was criss-crossed by a pair of cloth bandoliers. The overcoat had been looted from a shop near the College on the first evening of the rising, yet despite its protection he was obviously suffering. His hands were blue and he hugged himself, staring dead-eyed and unfocussed as he rocked back and forth.

"All right?" Liam asked anxiously.

"You bet."

A second later Kenny's cheeks ballooned and he ducked his head into the collar of the overcoat in an attempt to stifle a cough. Muffled, it shook his body from end to end and the dangling bandoliers swung like chains.

"Oh, Christ," he said quietly, the spasm ended.

The cough was worsening, and it posed a threat. Several times last night the choked sound of it had seemed certain to be heard by a passing patrol. Since daylight returned it had troubled him less, but the reprieve was only temporary; the bubbling whistle of his indrawn breath was growing audible again.

He spoke to Liam. "Remember us near the crossroads the other day?—when they used the eighteen-pounder and blew out the shop front just beyond?"

"I do."

2

"I was showered with lozenges then—paregoric, glycerine and honey. . . . There's irony for you. Like raindrops they were, spattering around."

"You should have filled your pockets."

"How was I to know?" An indecipherable emotion disturbed Kenny's expression. His face was as bare as a priest's and the effort of suppressing the cough had forced beads of sweat out on to his long upper lip. He seemed to become aware that Liam was watching him. "I'll be all right, don't worry."

"Sure you will."

"My sort take a lot of killing."

"Who said anything different?" Liam countered, and looked away. Bravado always made him feel uneasy.

They were in a sort of cave, except for not being completely roofed over. Floorboards partially covered the joists jutting above their heads, and now and again a gritty shower of dust spilled down from between the cracks. In places they could see the peeling rose-patterned wallpaper of the room immediately above them, in others an exposed section of broken staircase, elsewhere some dangling pipes and bomb-gashed plaster. Blast had somehow hooked an ivory-coloured chamber-pot on to the knobbed banister-rail of the staircase, and a small bright-painted statue of the Infant of Prague nestled in the gaping remains of a fireplace, intact and upside down.

These things vanished when night closed in: the cold intensified and the stars came pricking through with a gem-like glitter. It must have been about a couple of hours before dawn, the dawn before last, when Liam had led them scrambling into the ruined hotel. The Green had been eerily lit by flames and stabbing flashes and to begin with he had selected a vantage-point with a field of fire. Only with daylight's approach had he abandoned that position and in desperation led the others to where they were now.

The last orders he'd received were on no account to withdraw beyond the northern limits of the Green, and he was fatalist enough to believe that orders were to be obeyed to the letter. The fact that the given line had been overrun and by-passed became clear to them all soon after daybreak, but by that time it was too late even to contemplate a move. Someone in the same situation as themselves had taken the risk and was instantly caught by a machine-gun burst from a prowling armoured car. They had seen it happen, around eight in the morning and only fifty or sixty yards away, a youngish man in a dark blue cardigan; he was sprinting as the bullets smashed into him and they spun him round as though he were double-jointed.

Darkness had seemed to offer a chance of retreat. Liam remained reluctant, in two minds, but the others waited for nothing else, impatient and freezing and hungry. All day they had waited, listening to the ebb and flow of the fighting, sometimes dejected, sometimes encouraged. And then, as dusk began to thicken, they were dismayed to find that a searchlight was being moved into position near the bandstand.

"That's done it," Clodagh exclaimed, teeth clenched. "That's finished it for us."

Kenny swore. "You're easily beaten, you are." This was before the cold had entered into his marrow: he was game for anything then. Presently, when the piercing beam of light was switched on, he said: "We could shoot it out and make a dash. Up and over."

"No," Liam argued, crouching behind the rubble as the beam swivelled.

"One good aim and we'd have the thing as dead as a glass eye."

"No."

"Why not?"

"Where'd we make for?"

"Where? The river, of course."

Liam shook his head. "We wouldn't stand a chance. Not one chance in a hundred—dark or no. The position's changed, and for the worse. It's not what it was even an hour ago. You've only to listen. Between here and the river is overrun, overrun solid. We'd never make it—not the way things are. Besides, the last command Rogers gave was to stay put."

"Us and who else?"

"Stay put, he said. Lie low—like we've been doing."

"For how long, for Jesus' sake?"

"Until the situation's stabilized enough for counter-attacks to be mounted."

"That could mean for ever," Clodagh said bitterly. "We should have—"

"I'm telling you what Rogers wanted of us. If we were outflanked or isolated we were to go to earth. Those were his very words—go to earth."

"What happens if the counter-attacks fail?"

"They won't." Liam hesitated: there was more at stake than themselves. "They mustn't."

"But if they do?"

"Why press it?" Liam snapped. The shadows swirled and congealed as the searchlight probed. "I tell you again, we're best off where we are. If we tried to work north now

we'd last no more than minutes, singly or together. . . .
Wait, that's what I say." He paused. He had never wished to
command. "Don't you see, Kenny?"

"Maybe."

"We aren't the only ones. There'll be others the same
as us, hiding up. God knows there are places enough.
We'll come into our own yet."

"Maybe," Kenny conceded.

"Clodagh?"

She said nothing.

"We're staying, Clodagh. And that's an order."

Night-long they had huddled in the darkness, lying
together, hearing the soft drip-drip-drip from the tap that
punctuated the passage of time, listening to the wheeze
strengthen in Kenny's lungs, tense and fearful when he
tried to bury his cough in his shoulder. Sometimes they
drifted into sleep: exhausted though they were it was
never more than shallow and was frequently disturbed.
On and off the rattle of small-arms' fire or the crump of
an explosion sounded from the direction of the river.
Occasionally it was closer than the river and their hopes
fluttered, but in vain.

The searchlight fingered the buildings around the Green,
shining deep into their exposed insides, illuminating the
streets that led north and west and east, now dawdling, now
swinging swiftly from point to point, now suddenly holding
still. Silence seemed to intensify wherever the beam fell,
but once—around midnight—there was shouting and the
light stopped eagerly in its tracks and a machine-gun
opened up, spraying the alley beside the dairy. There
were a couple of sharp bursts as something moved, then
slumped. Quiet settled again.

"A dog," Liam whispered, peering.

The sense of anticlimax shamed him. For a few heart-thudding seconds it had seemed that he was vindicated, that others *were* nearby. He had almost willed the machine-gun to be answered by a defiant stammer of rifle-fire, if only to prove that he and Kenny and Clodagh were not alone.

"A dog," he repeated.

Kenny craned his thin neck. "Just as well."

"Dog, cat," Clodagh breathed. "What else could it have been?"

"Listen," Liam hissed at her. "Why in the name of God d'you suppose they use the searchlight? For amusement?— is that what you think? For practice? So as to make a study of the damage and ruin their shells have made?"

His mind prickled. "There's none so blind," his mother always used to say, "as those who don't want to see."

"They're on the watch for infiltration by our lads into the areas on either side of the Green. It's like a rabbit-warren there, whichever side you go, and they're using the light to augment their patrols. They can shine it right along some of those streets. Sure, the fighting's gone round behind our backs for a while, but that doesn't mean they have this district finally safe—and they're aware of that."

Kenny came to his support. "What Liam says makes sense."

"Since when were you first with a gun in your hand?" Clodagh countered.

"Friday last, the same as you, the same as Liam."

"Five days," she said. "Five days, and already he's speaking like a general and you're believing him."

"He makes sense, that's why."

"Then answer me this, then."

"Answer you what?"

"If there's a danger to them of infiltration, as Liam puts it, how can he also say it isn't possible for us to quit where we are and reach the river?"

"Because," Liam cut in, "those weren't Rogers' instructions." He paused, hugging himself against the nauseous cold. It wasn't a time to argue. "For the sake of us all, Clodagh, curb your impatience and your tongue. I'm no general. Until last week I taught in school."

She couldn't let go. "And they listened?"

"I was in charge," he said. "Like now."

Dawn had been a long grey smear, slow to brighten. The searchlight was extinguished and dragged behind the bandstand. Little by little the Green disclosed its scars, the hard white frost, the leafless trees, everything motionless. Gradually the morning had gained colour and the three of them could see themselves again, not speaking their thoughts, scarcely speaking at all, lying curled as if in the womb. The sounds of fighting reached them in snatches from the north; it was crisp, like ice cracking, but no nearer than before.

Clodagh had been the first to stir, stiffly making a long arm to replace the fragment of shattered wall-mirror on the rubble's crest. The glass was only a few square inches in area, but Liam had insisted she took it down when the searchlight came into action. By day it was invaluable, a safe eye with which to observe without risking exposure.

"Anything?" Liam said.

"There's some coming and going at the far end, near where the tram-car is."

He watched the tightness, the hatred, in her face. "Let me see."

She relinquished her position and he tilted his head, eyes narrowed, studying the distant reflected figures uniformed in black and khaki, hating them himself, needing nothing to aid him in that but living memory yet sharing with Clodagh a sense of communion with dead generations.

"They're in at the baker's there."

An avalanche of dust spilled without warning from the staircase edge. Kenny spluttered and rolled sideways, jerking as he muffled the cough, retching. Liam urgently scanned the Green, dreading the sight of someone within earshot; if their presence in the ruins was even suspected they were as good as finished.

"Use the tap," he urged Kenny.

Kenny crawled to the bath and cupped his mottled hands, frail and haggard as he drank. "It's heat I'm wanting. Inside myself." He tried to grin, offering it like an apology. "If someone lighted a cigarette for me now I believe I'd eat the thing."

By noon a pallid sun had lifted the frost from the ground. By noon, too, Liam had pinpointed the look-out post above the baker's shop and concluded that street barriers had been erected in most of the east and west exits from the Green. The barriers themselves weren't visible, but he had watched a couple of trucks shuttle back and forth, one carrying wire and trestles, the other armed working-parties. It was disturbing to note their casualness and the increased confidence of the patrols. Only men who believed they were in a safe rear area would have dared to carry their rifles slung; and, for the most part, these men did.

He fretted. Was he naive to have taken Rogers at his

naked word, as some took the Bible, with no questions asked? Left to himself his faith in a counter-attack and its outcome would have remained unshaken. As it was he found himself undermined by Kenny's physical deterioration and Clodagh's carping. When they were first together he had sought to shield her. It was unimaginable to fight alongside a woman—a girl, really; twenty, his guess was—and to have her ask no favours. Or to lie beside her as close as a husband and share hunger and danger and cold on equal terms. He wasn't prepared for what she was.

"Can you load a rifle?"

"Like this, you mean?"

She had snapped the five rounds into the magazine with a single downward pressure of her right thumb. This was in the yard behind Hafferty's place when they were grouping together, and she did it more efficiently than he'd even managed himself.

"God," he'd said in admiration, "you're quick to learn."

"My father showed me how."

"Does he have a Lee-Enfield?"

"He did have," she said cryptically.

He didn't know about her father at that stage. There were a thousand things he didn't know—about her, about Kenny—and they hadn't been his concern. All he was sure of was the fact that chance had put a woman in his charge, and it was second nature to assume he would have to shield her. Even after the ambush near the bank, when she was calmer and more deadly than any of them, he had continued to be protective. It must have taken him a full two days to grasp that she could fend for herself, unflinching and without complaint amid the screaming and the blasphemies and the splintering screech of fragmented metal.

The action at the crossroads was behind them by then. After the crossroads the initiative had begun to slip away and they were forced more and more on to the defensive. For a while it hadn't seemed so; the murderous house-to-house shambles between the big picture-palace and the Green had swung unevenly in the balance, but rifles and hand-grenades were no lasting match against field-guns firing over open sights and the relentless mobility of armoured cars.

"Go to earth," Rogers commanded hoarsely, crouching with about a score of section leaders behind a church wall. "Stay put, whatever happens on your flanks."

Spent and deafened they had come into this demolished place like hunted people. Years seemed to have passed through Liam's brain. They had stumbled out of a nightmare of flashes and explosions and entered into an intensity of silence and furtive inaction. And Clodagh couldn't endure what it entailed. The cold, yes; the hunger, yes. But not the passive waiting.

"We'll move, surely?"—this within hours, while his mind was still grey with exhaustion.

"No."

By tacit agreement they went behind the bath to relieve themselves, but there were no other proprieties. She was dressed like a man and had shown herself bolder than many, superior with a rifle to most. Liam had ceased to feel protective towards her; if anyone needed shielding it was beginning to be Kenny. But whereas Kenny's condition was likely to worsen, Liam had felt he could at least impose on Clodagh a necessary degree of discipline.

"There'll be no shooting," he warned early on. "And no showing your head above the top of the rubble there.

Rig up a periscope with a bit of mirror, but that's all."

"And then what?"

"Rest." He lifted his shoulders. "Pray." He meant it.

"I don't need telling about prayer."

She had fine rebellious eyes, wide-set and full of expression: they smouldered when she was corrected. For all her resilience she was on the slight side, of medium height. God knows where she had got the trousers from, but they were tight on her; the tunic, too, split under the armpits.

"Mind you don't need telling about anything."

She would learn in time, he thought. He had still believed she would learn right up until their second imprisoned afternoon when, incredulously, he had seen her reach for the rifle and squirm up the slope of rubble. For a long moment he had watched dumbfounded, mind and body temporarily dissociated as she steadied and took aim. An enormous effort was required to break the spell and go in a frenzy after her.

"*Idiot!*"

It was then that he witnessed the look that he was never to fathom, the one that frightened him. They had fought a silent battle with their eyes, whole worlds of incomprehension locked together in mutual dismay.

"He was a dead man. I had him. . . ."

Mother of God, he thought, and alarm fingered his spine. It was unbelievable that anyone should be so single-minded.

"Do that again," he threatened gravely after giving her back the rifle, "and I'll wring your neck—d'you hear?"

She looked away.

"I promise you," he said, and his voice trembled. "This is war we're in, not a private vendetta."

And for the one and only time of his knowing her something like a soft-lipped smile shaped the corners of her pale mouth.

2

ANOTHER DUSK BEGAN to thicken. The day had seemed everlasting, but dusk itself was swift, shrinking distances, merging one thing into another.

The searchlight cradle was trundled into position again and Liam took the fragment of mirror down before the blinding white beam was turned on. The sound of gunfire had come no closer and was sometimes dishearteningly thin. If he hadn't heard Rogers with his own ears it would have been even easier to despair.

He lay on his back and watched the statuette of the Infant of Prague dissolve into the dark. He was weak and sometimes dizzy from lack of food. Despite the cold he felt feverish. There were also cramping pains in his belly, yet he listened to the reedy whistling from Kenny's heaving chest with increasing anxiety, tinged with guilt and misgivings.

"What brought you into this, Kenny?" They were strangers even now.

"I wasn't going to be the only one to stay home." It was as if he had a harmonica buried deep in his lungs. "One in, all in—that's the Doyles. There's four brothers besides me, and half of them are dab hands with explosives. Every time I hear a loudish thump I tell myself it's them— D.V."

"What's your work?"

"Drayman," Kenny wheezed. "With the brewery."

The light idled over their part of the hotel, silencing them, allowing them a shadowy glimpse of themselves—Clodagh with her knees drawn under her chin, Kenny's mouth hanging open, Liam with the back of his cap down almost to his eyes. There was a kind of indifference about the way in which the light probed, as if those behind it weren't as watchful as before and no longer saw the need to be; cordons were across the side streets and movement about the Green had been demonstrably safe since afternoon.

Liam burrowed his chin under his buttoned jacket so as to trap the warmth of his breath.

"Have you a family?" To his surprise it was Clodagh.

"Not of my own," he said. "Not any more."

"Married, were you?"

"That's right."

The knife twisted in his heart again. The view from a window filled his mind's eye—fields laid between low stone walls, moss and lichen streaked on limestone, cattle grazing beneath trees. "She's dead, Liam. . . . The child as well. It was all too much for her." Four years ago this was, and nothing had ever been quite the same, or could be. "Why me?" he'd asked her once, stricken with sudden wonder. "What made you choose me?" And ever since he'd carried her laughing answer with him: "Choose? Liam Gallagher, in love there *is* no choosing."

He ran his tongue over his bad teeth, listening in the darkness to the footfalls of an approaching patrol, praying to God that Kenny's cough wouldn't surface and betray their presence: his breathing alone was almost loud enough. It was the usual two-man patrol, but whereas they had last night roamed in silence now they talked between themselves, the voices thick, the accents alien.

When they were almost level with the hotel they stopped. Liam stiffened. There was the scrape of a grounded rifle-butt. "Fag?" a voice said. Simultaneously he felt Clodagh stir. In haste he checked her, grabbing and taking hold of an arm; he didn't trust her any more. With immense caution he raised himself over the parapet, inching his head above the top. The two men were barely fifty feet away, standing close, one with his hands cupped around a match as both lit up; for a moment the faces were bright orange and the long bayonets gleamed.

The searchlight came swinging round, beginning to silhouette the pair in advance of it reaching them, and Liam ducked. Kenny's breathing was like a kettle nearing the boil. The beam stroked across smashed walls and rafters and the bathroom seemed to spin on an axis as it passed.

Liam raised his head again, willing the patrol to move away, beginning to sweat for fear of Kenny's cough erupting. Every second was stretching elastically into unbearable lengths of time. For Christ's sake, he urged, watching the cigarettes glow like fireflies. Whole minutes must have elapsed. Great heaps of rubble had spilled over the pavements and the two men stood well out into the roadway, stamping their feet. One of them muttered something and his companion chuckled. "Come on," he said eventually, and relief swept Liam like a breaker.

He'd been temporarily oblivious of the cold; now, as the footsteps started to recede, he cringed from it. For a while he remained gazing after the retreating patrol, just his cap and eyes showing. Then gingerly he lowered himself to where the others were and curled in close to them.

"Gone," he whispered, although they must have known.

Kenny began to cough almost as though he'd been given a signal. The muffled, half-choked noise seemed worse than ever. His lungs were bubbling again and the night was hardly started; by Liam's watch it was only eight o'clock. When the coughing finally ended Kenny let out a kind of rasping sigh.

"Do you really believe it, Liam?"

"Believe what?"

"That we aren't the only squad still by the Green?"

"Of course."

"That others are holed up like ourselves?"

"I'm sure."

"We haven't been stranded then, high and dry?"

"Never."

Clodagh began: "If you ask me—"

"I'm not asking you."

"To blazes with that," she said.

A single shot sounded in the far distance, as if a sniper had somewhere chanced his arm.

"I'm asking Liam," Kenny laboured. "He was the one who got it from Rogers, and I want to believe we're here for a reason." His teeth clattered as if they were loose in his mouth. "I *have* to believe it. Tell me it's only a matter of time, Liam."

"So it is."

"On your heart you're saying that?"

"Would I lie to you?"

Now in the self-same distance a machine-gun yapped.

"I'm on fire," Kenny complained. "Ice and fire. . . . Tomorrow, d'you reckon? D'you reckon we'll be counter-attacking by the morning?"

"With luck," Liam said doggedly.

When they came blundering frantically into the ruins he had thought in terms of being pinned down for hours. Hours, not days and nights. Thirst had consumed him then; the taste of fear was in his throat and hunger belonged to the future. Now his guts groaned and he was light in the head and Kenny was on his way to pneumonia or something; God alone knew.

He gazed up at the stars and trembled with them, besieged by doubts, wretched and uncertain. His faith in Rogers' ability to match his word was beginning gradually to crumble. An attack should have come in well before this time, and in another twenty-four hours it would probably be too late. By morning? . . . He wished he was half as confident as he made out.

Whenever the searchlight swivelled past he could see frost hardening on the level surfaces around them. We should have gone, he thought. We should have shot the thing blind and made a dash for it, like Kenny said. Scattered. A quarter of a mile to the river—we might have made it, some of us anyhow; there were alleys enough, back ways, broken places, rooftops even. Better than staying put.

Staying put was never to have been like this. Sooner or later without support it could only mean the end of them, an isolated flurry. He had no illusions; they could expect no mercy.

He closed his eyes, on edge, urging calmness into himself. Hindsight was a terrible affliction. Hafferty's yard had been a lottery, and of all the people there he'd drawn a sick man and a rebel of a girl, probably the only woman in the place.

"Are you from the west?"

"What if I am?" she said.

"I'm only asking."

"Once upon a time."

"What's that supposed to mean?"

"Whatever you want to make of it."

For days he had been detached, intent only on keeping the three of them together.

"Don't you ever give anything away about yourself?"

"It's better not to."

"Is that what you think?"

"Why else would I be saying it?"

She moved in the darkness, their legs touching, a hand mistakenly pressing against his hip.

"Is your safety-catch on?"

"Of course."

"Check," he said.

"There's no need."

"Check," he said grimly, "or I'll kick the lard out of you. If there's one thing we don't need now it's a round going off."

"D'you suppose I'm a fool?"

"You were this afternoon. A leopard doesn't change its spots, not to my knowledge."

A flare lifted lazily into the sky; they saw it drift across a jagged star-filled gap above where the staircase was.

"Which means," she said after a pause, "we're here for good."

"It doesn't follow."

"By the same token it does. *Per omnia saecula saeculorum.*"

"No."

"Then what's keeping us?"

She was baiting him and he knew it.

"Orders," she said with derision.

He held his tongue, immense and incommunicable experiences both a bond and a barrier between them.

"Wishful thinking's nearer the mark. . . . Rogers and his pockets of resistance—Jesus!"

"Another twenty-four hours will decide. All it wants is—"

"A miracle, that's what it wants. What are you trying to prove?"

"Prove?—nothing. We were given a job to do, and as long—"

"D'you call this a job? Hiding." She was scornful. "We should have got out while there was a chance. Kenny thought so too. But oh no." There was a razor-sharp silence, long and lasting, just Kenny's ugly breathing and no more. Her mouth was inches away as she whispered: "If you think he can take another twenty-four hours like this—"

"Shut up!"

"Unless something's done—"

"Don't listen to her, Kenny boy."

"You'll be the death of him, you will."

He struck at her blindly, appalled and enraged, making only glancing contact. "Since when did you start caring? What about the afternoon? We'd all have been for the high jump if you'd had your way."

"Stop it," Kenny pleaded, his voice so hushed it was almost no voice at all.

Clodagh wasn't finished. "You can't bring yourself to face the truth, that's your trouble."

"Listen to me—"

"*Stop it!*"

Liam glared into the blackness, a pulsing vibration behind his eyes. Shame spread through him as the moments passed. He covered his stubbled face with freezing hands, consumed by an enormous feeling of remorse and impotence. His mind seemed to go beyond the limits of coherence into an awful throbbing vacancy. He remained like that for what seemed a long time, listening to the whining chords that came from Kenny's lungs, knowing that from now on they would be to him a persistent accusation.

Four days ago, after a skirmish before dawn amid an odorous hugger-mugger of slums and railway sidings, Clodagh had picked off a Lewis-gunner positioned on a low roof as surely as if it were daylight. Liam was beside her when it happened.

"You must have eyes like an owl," he'd said, amazed.

"It was easy."

"I'd lost him since the flashes."

"Easier still if there'd been phosphorus on the foresight."

"Phosphorus?"

"You only need a blob."

"Who taught you that one?"

"My father.

"What else did this father of yours teach you?"

"Who to respect."

Later he came to ask himself whether hatred had been

34

implanted in her before or after her father's death. They'd executed him; found arms and documents in the house and walked him out and shot him on the spot—that much she'd volunteered. But whether the trauma of this one act had turned her into a killer or whether the instinct had been fostered, he couldn't have said. There was elemental savagery and there was innocence. He'd glimpsed both, and the combination disturbed him in a way that didn't bear thinking about, alarm drawn across his soul.

On top of everything else time was proving her right. Nine o'clock passed, ten o'clock came and went, and with every hour their position grew a shade more hopeless. Desultory exchanges crackled in the vicinity of the river, but nothing was intense or sustained enough to indicate an approaching attack; if anything there was a lull. The tap dripped, measuring off the night with the precision of a metronome, and the searchlight wandered slowly without pause. A little after ten Kenny suddenly began to sing under his breath, the tune breaking on his lips like bubbles:

"At the risin' of the moon,
At the risin' of the moon,
For the pikes must be together
At the risin' of the moon. . . ."

"Don't, Kenny boy. Save yourself."

"By morning, you said?" He sounded odd, like a child.

"God between us and all harm."

It was awful to be trusted. Sleep plucked at Liam despite the rack of his nerves and the freezing cold. He never thought he quite went under; always he seemed to be aware of the others, Kenny in particular but Clodagh as well. Once, as if in a dream, he imagined he saw her face, pale beyond words, the cheeks hollow, the eyes wide. A wind was blowing, a brown wind, stripping the trees. He was aware it was hallucination, yet he somehow believed he retained full consciousness. She walked towards him through the scudding rain of leaves and it was only when they had come quite close that he realized he was staring into the memory of another time and that it wasn't her at all.

Something snapped in him. He sat up sharply, reality in the wheezing and his own gnawing emptiness. The wheezing was very bad now, like air blown into water through a straw. He shifted cautiously, taking hold of his rifle, the metal icy to the touch. He uncoiled himself and clambered up the breast of rubble that shielded them on the open side. The beam of the searchlight was stationary, aimed into one of the exits off to the right, and the bare trees lining the paths across the Green stood out as stark and black as iron.

It was twenty past eleven and clouds were beginning to mask the stars. The vivid horizontal bar of light intensified the surrounding darkness. Liam could see nothing that wasn't in silhouette, though almost as soon as he raised his head a staff car swept into view in direct line with the bandstand and its headlamps briefly exposed the damage to the Green's south-east corner. A florist's and a bookstore were what he best remembered at that end, but now there were caverns and freakish remnants of inner and outer walls, from which a charcoal pillar of smoke had risen until yesterday.

He tried to recall what made up the northern frontage to the Green. Even in daylight a sidelong view was obstructed by debris; in places entire buildings had spewed outwards. Vaguely he could remember a tea-shop, though its exact location defeated him; he wasn't often in the city.

There was also a milliner's somewhere, and a grocer's. In his mind he crossed to the Green itself and stared back at where he was, picturing the hotel and the four-storeyed Georgian terrace extending to either side. The tea-shop was a dozen or so premises away, and the grocer's was further away still. In between was an office of some kind—insurance, was it?—and a corn chandler's: he could only guess at the others.

Hunger had sharpened his senses. The dragging sound of marching men came to him from the near distance, out of a street somewhere. From the opposite direction, north-wards, he heard the death-rattle of automatic fire, and another flare burst in the sky like the last of the stars come down to bloom. One of the searchlight crew cleared his throat and spat. All around amongst the ruins there were constantly small avalanches and the warning creak of unstable pressures. And closest of all there was Kenny, always Kenny, deteriorating by the hour.

Liam thought of the shops again, prodded by desperation, wondering what remained. There was a pub, too, surely?— *The Saloon*. "That's no name to have called it by," his father had once grumbled. "How can it be anything decent with a mediocre name like that?" *The Saloon*, yes—some-where in the vicinity of the chemist's.

God, the chemist's ... MacSweeney—gilt lettering on a green fascia: how the mind worked.

He chewed his lower lip. Chemist, pub, grocer—was it conceivable that one of these might have survived, even in part, without being completely picked clean? Soon after they had reached this broken derelict place he'd endeavoured to make his way into the hotel's interior, hoping to find blankets, spare clothing, food even. But in vain; no proper interior remained. It was impossible to go higher, and everything on or below their level that might have warmed or protected them was buried under mountains of ruin. When he crawled cautiously about there were collapses and cavings-in which threatened to give their position away. So he had settled for conditions as they were and the privations they entailed, blinkered by the prospect of an early counter-attack.

Until now. His latest clash with Clodagh had awakened him to the fact that Kenny was hastening to a crisis. Three hours later it was obvious, undeniable. Against his will he was being forced to admit the need for urgency. The coughing had constantly threatened their existence, and did so still, but it seemed to Liam now that the situation had gone beyond mere extremes of hardship.

To be killed was one thing; but to die, to be *allowed* to die. . . . The sense of guilt returned. All at once inaction was a crime. Liam shivered, looking blankly at the Green, struggling to revive the power of decision, thinking back thinking forward.

"It's heat I'm wanting . . . Inside myself"—the memory echoed, urging him to move.

He heard Clodagh pull herself beside him. "What is it?"

"Nothing."

"You've been as still as a gun-dog."

Their breath rose like mist. "How well d'you know the Green?"

"I don't," she answered.

"Not at all?"

"From picture-books, maybe. Why?"

"I was wondering."

The searchlight slewed through twenty degrees, then focussed like a burning-glass on a gap in a wall.

"About Kenny, is it?"

"Yes."

"Kenny's not up to taking to his heels, if that's what you've got in mind."

"It isn't."

"Last night he could have chanced it, but not any more." Salt in the wound; she rubbed it in. "It's too late for him now."

"Don't *say* that!"

"Making a dash, I mean."

"It's help he needs—that's what I'm on about. Something to tide him over . . . Warmth, food." Liam paused, indicating the destruction along the sides of the Green. "I've been thinking. Across there doesn't look up to much, and even if it were possible for me to make it I don't suppose—"

"You?"

"Me, yes."

"Leaving here?" Surprise thickened her whisper. "You?"

"That's right. But keeping to this end."

"You're off your head."

"There were shops along this end. Tea-shop, grocer, chemist—"

"Were," she said.

"Others I've forgotten. A pub as well."

"Yesterday," she reminded him, "they loaded a lorry. Bales of cloth—down by the near corner. You saw them yourself."

"What of it?"

"They won't have left a thing anywhere. Thieves, that's what they are. Thieves, drunkards—"

"I know what they are." Something scurried invisibly nearby, pit-a-pat. "No need to tell me."

"If anything's standing they'll have cleaned it out, sure to God they will."

"Have they come looking in the hotel?" he protested.

"No."

"Well, then."

"It isn't worth their while, that's why."

"If I ferret around it could pay off."

"You've left it late."

"To eat my words?"

"I didn't say that."

"He's gone downhill all of a sudden. Besides—"

Liam stopped, not wanting to war with her again. They had survived so much—and might survive more yet. Freely and with his eyes open he'd chosen to rendezvous at Hafferty's yard; at best he'd only some left-over life to lose. But with others it was different. Pity stirred in him as he listened to Kenny's throttled panting. Amid the bright strands of personal courage those lapses into bravado had always struck him as ill-fated.

You did all right, his mind said. Great. Never fear about that, Kenny.

"When will you go?"

"The sooner the better," he said.

"Is it after midnight?"

"About twenty to."

"How long will you be?"

"How can I say? Are you daft? It depends."

"Will you be taking your gun?"

He shook his head, though she wasn't aware of it.

"Will you?"

"No." It was extraordinary, but he sensed concern. "What is it?"

"You wouldn't be dumping us, would you?"

"I don't understand."

"Quitting."

"Are you daft?" he said again, surprised as much as hurt. "A deserter—is that how you see me?"

"No."

"What's your worry, then?"

She hesitated; it was unlike her. He had never for an instant suspected her of being capable of weakness or uncertainty. Much of what she acted upon was mercilessly clear-cut—so much so that often, amid pains and apprehensions of his own, he forgot that she was only a girl and little more than half his age.

"How could I leave Kenny?"

They were very close as he whispered, their heads almost touching. What he said was offered as a kind of guarantee, yet it offended her. He was too much within himself to care very much, but he felt her hostility at once and with rough tenderness he gripped her by the shoulder.

"If I don't return," he tried again, "it won't be of my own choosing."

She pulled away from him. Wild thing, he thought dismissively, and raised himself chest-high over the rubble so as to be able to see where first to make for. The searchlight was beamed on the Green's east side and there was no sign anywhere of a patrol. "It's raining cough-drops," Kenny burbled suddenly.

In his temples Liam could feel his pulse quickening against the rim of his cap. He wedged his rifle in a firm place and rid himself of the half-empty bandoliers, looping them over the muzzle. The sky was completely covered now, the clouds like pack-ice.

"Listen, Clodagh."

She said nothing.

"No madness. Don't open up on anyone, whatever you do, no matter how tempting." He thought he saw her eyes, silver-white in the hollows of shadow. "And keep your fingers crossed."

"Is that an order?"

"Oh, to hell with you," Liam snapped.

The sound of Kenny's gasping was about his ears. As quickly and quietly as he could he reached the crest of the parapet and started over its forward slope, crouching, steadying himself with his hands. After more than two days of being hemmed in he felt terribly exposed. The tip of rubble that filled the open side of the bathroom sloped in a conic-shaped section all the way down and out to the pavement below. He worked sideways across it, edging lower, watching the searchlight. By the time it came jerking round he was at street-level, pressing into a crevasse of debris, Kenny's struggle for breath substituted by a version of his own.

3

He was dreadfully weak. Sometimes he seemed to lack the ability to check himself from going off balance. Once, when he grabbed to keep steady, whatever he dislodged slithered for seconds on end. He flattened and waited, unnerved, but the searchlight didn't come back to investigate and after a while he moved cautiously on.

The building towered above him and the rubble was heaped like dunes. As soon as he could he found a way inside, but where he was he didn't know. Some kind of room, linoleum under broken glass. He could hardly see and he fumbled forward, groping, stealthily transferring his weight from one foot to the other. There was a decaying smell and a wall was missing, floorboards gone. He backed clear and discovered stone steps leading down, iron palings set at an angle. This time he edged away, fearing a drop into a basement. Scattered blocks of masonry hid him from the

Green and he felt round past them, every granular crunch and jarring tremor plucking at his nerves.

Kenny and Clodagh had already receded in the face of his own stark vulnerability. In a straight line he reckoned he had covered about twenty yards from the bathroom. For certain he was past the hotel; his eyes had adjusted and there was a general reflected glimmer which wasn't in evidence until he got outside. He went on all fours across a tangle of crashed slates and guttering, the frost white and treacherous. Where had he thought the tea-shop was? He peered to his right, confused and despairing. It was lunacy to have supposed anything might be intact after such concentrated shelling and the fires that followed it. Yet it was equally unthinkable that he should accept defeat so soon and return empty-handed.

The quiet was like a living thing holding its breath in expectation of his clumsiness. He kept close in, the freakish remains of Georgian elegance like a broken bluff above him, dark and crumbled or hollowed-out or spilled away from itself. There was nothing yet to indicate the existence of a shop, any shop. He threaded in and out of several private houses in succession, each with railings guarding a basement area, the basements choked, the ground floors impassable. In the fourth house, to the side of where the front door must once have been, he stumbled over something, and when he bent to identify what it was he touched a raincoat, then a man, dead, rigid, hair like wire, arms twisted under him, a rifle by his legs.

"We haven't been stranded then, high and dry?" Kenny's whisper echoed like a frightened child's. We have, he thought. Oh Christ, yes. . . . Suddenly the weakness in him was more than physical. The dead and the absent were all one. He

44

lurched out into the dark chaos of the street, filled with a terrifying loneliness. An empty can went clattering. Instantly the light came swinging his way, eager again, flickering clockwise and at speed through the bare black branches of the trees.

He collapsed as silently as his strength allowed, half rolling as he fell—knees, hip, shoulder. The beam swept by, wavered, then started slowly back, sending the shadows into reverse. He pressed against the pavement behind the remnants of a fallen balcony, his heart like a pile-driver on the stone. The acetylene dazzle poured above and to both sides of him, inches away, glittering on the pavement slabs. He shut his eyes against its brilliance, motionless, believing he must have been seen, panic rising as the long moments passed. All the time he was losing the hold on himself not to make a break, and all the time he kept thinking of the dog and the machine-gun bursts.

Lord have mercy, Christ have mercy ... the gabble had started in his mind when the blinding whiteness chased elsewhere. He remained where he was, a thin sweat oozing out of him, the dark blood-red and shaky. A couple of minutes must have elapsed before he could trust himself to move again. He levered himself up and went on, the hunted feeling deep and destructive, hopelessness gaining ground.

There was a shop here, or what remained of one— FLANAGAN; the name-board jutted like a fin from a hump of brick and stone, and Liam finger-traced the embossed lettering. Bits of furniture were everywhere embedded in the rubble—chairs, a sofa ... lampshades, were they? Nothing seemed exactly real, almost as if a nightmare had somehow overflowed into life, and every tiny snapping sound that marked his progress seemed to be amplified by the bitter cold and to race tell-tale across the Green.

A whiff of gas hung on the air. There were other shops now, a row of them, gutted, still filled with the clinging tang of smoke and ashes. He explored from one to another, crawling, scrabbling softly and without success in the charred flotsam. A patrol passed within a few yards of him and he lay as stiff as dead until it had gone. He saw the two men clearly in profile—the tam-o'-shanter berets singling them out for the mercenaries that they were, newcomers, the worst of enemies.

Relief dragged at the corners of his mouth as the slow footsteps went away. Presently he found a length of velvet curtain. To begin with he couldn't decide what its softness was, but well before he'd finished unearthing it he knew it would do as a covering for Kenny. In the darkness he spiked it on a railing, trying to memorize the railing's precise whereabouts. The curtain was all he had to show for half an hour's searching, and it mocked him. "You're off your head"—Clodagh had made no bones about his chances of success.

A wave of dizziness surged through him. His mind was in tatters and he wasn't able to control the ricochet course of his thoughts. Kenny's condition had called his judgment into question and the sense of personal failure was mounting all the time. Being out here was as futile as it was desperate. Kenny needed impossible things—medicines, nourishment, nursing—and out here there wasn't a crumb, not even a tea-shop's leftovers or anything anywhere. Nor was there likely to be. MacSweeney's, *The Saloon*, a grocer's—he might as well have imagined them all. And yet he still couldn't bring himself to consider making his way uselessly back to the hotel. All that would then stand between them and ultimate disaster was a dawn counter-attack and he had hoped for an attack for so long that it was hard to hope again; madness.

The piece of curtain was only a beginning. Somewhere there had to be food. *Had to be.* . . . The words floated like a challenge in the numbness of his brain.

Mostly there was silence from the curve of the river. If Rogers was regrouping he must hurry. What had once been a head-on battle had gradually separated into a series of skirmishes, lacking focus or co-ordination. In the bathroom they had listened to the change, the two-day dying away. Now an individual sniper let fly or a few random exchanges shook the frost-white stillness, but this was all—and it was ominously at a distance, more like defeat than a lull.

Liam emptied his mind of Rogers, unreasoningly soured by the thought of him, the feeling of abandonment prickling his senses. He crept on, approaching a corner where a street led northwards. In between were great undulations of rubble and he could make out patches of sky through some of the buildings. Was this *The Saloon?*—at the end here?

He sculled forward with his elbows, pressing low as the searchlight meandered round. A lorry was coming along the street toward the Green and he made urgently for a basement. It was like a trench, with steps down from pavement level. He backed in, listening to the lorry rattling up the street. The searchlight swung in greeting and as the lorry emerged into view the driver protested with the horn.

"Douse it, you! . . . Get away!"—the raucous Cockney voices rose from a load of soldiers. "Stupid bugger, what d'you reckon you're doing?"

The searchlight careered elsewhere, joke over, and the lorry took the right-angle turn. Liam flattened as it went by, and missed his footing. For a second or so he struggled to save himself, the noise drowned by the passing lorry: then he fell heavily into the space below—four, five feet, though it seemed more. He jarred his right hip and shoulder, face contorted, fearing worse. But there was no pain, nothing serious, only a sense of tumult in his head as the lorry passed along the length of the Green.

He straightened up, in a pit, the blackness intense, a narrow rectangle of sky smeared overhead. And then, invisible yet very close, someone spoke and his skin crawled with fright.

"One move," this someone said. "One move, whoever you are, and it'll be your last."

Liam held his breath, eyes straining.

"Who are you?"

The accent emboldened him. "That cuts both ways."

"*Cad as tu?*" Menace in the tone. "Where are you from?"

"*Faigh amach.* Find out."

Distrust remained despite the Gaelic. "Are you armed?"

"No."

"I'm not as blind as you, remember."

"I am not armed," Liam said with care. Shock still trembled in him.

"I am," the other said.

"I believe you."

"I've got a shotgun and it's a foot from your head. You're wearing a cap."

"Correct."

48

"Do as I say, then."

"Very well."

Softly, softly, every word. "There's a window-ledge in front of you. Feel for it, then step over and through. The glass is all gone."

Liam swung his legs across the sill. His boots gritted on sagging floorboards.

"Straight ahead of yourself," the voice said. "Six or seven paces and you'll find a door."

"I'm there," Liam said presently.

"Open it and wait the other side."

He did so. The door was shut again. The space was enclosed, narrow and he could feel the other person, smell his breath and sharp ammoniac sweat.

"There's another door."

Liam fumbled for the knob. Candle-light greeted him as the door yielded. Stupefied, he stood stock still, face screwed. A second man was there, behind a table, revolver raised.

"Jesus to God," the man said, lowering the revolver. "Who's this?"

"He was outside. I thought it was maybe someone stalking us."

"Outside? Where outside?"

"At the bottom of the steps."

"I fell," Liam said. His thoughts were racing in all directions. "A lorry went by and I took cover. Ask your friend."

The man with the revolver was Kenny's age, stocky, dark-haired, red-faced, veins broken in the skin. The other one was younger, leaner, eager-eyed, both hands clamped on the shotgun.

"He fell, right enough."

"What were you doing out there?"

"Searching," Liam said.

His teeth chattered uncontrollably. The very slight warmth of the place seemed to draw the spasm from him. His vision clouded and his knees sagged. He gripped the edge of the table, bewildered, head down, weakness and relief and amazement tossing in the convulsions of his mind.

"Here—try this."

It was whiskey. With a kind of disbelief he tilted the bottle and swallowed.

"Searching?"

He nodded.

"What for?"

He couldn't answer right away. "Food."

"Where did you make a start from?"

They were patient with him and allowed him time.

"Tonight, you mean?"

"Tonight, yes."

He hesitated, wits smothered by events. "This end of the Green."

"How long have you been at this end?"

"Two days." The whiskey was like a flame inside him. "Over forty-eight hours."

"And before that?"

"The picture-palace." He gestured vaguely. "The crossroads. . . . The bank."

"And first of all?"

The low ceiling was pressing down on him. "First of all we were behind Hafferty's place."

It was like a password. The older man raised the bottle. "*Slaun lath.*" Then he held out a hand, they both did, and

Liam shook them. "Tell me," the same man said, "are you the one who's been doing the tapping?"

"Tapping?"

"On a pipe."

"No."

"So there's someone else—besides you and us, I mean."

Emotion constricted Liam's throat. "I . . . I thought everyone else was either dead or gone. Everything pointed to it. One of our lot's ill . . . past moving, and there's only water where we are. God, it's seemed so hopeless, and on top of the rest—"

He broke off, moved beyond words. He closed his eyes and steadied himself, knuckles bone-white as he gripped the table, He had forgotten what warmth was.

"Tell me," he began again, but managed no more. Disbelief was still not far away. His gaze jerked round the filthy cellar-like space. Rickety table, solitary chair, single mattress in the corner on the stone floor—there wasn't much to take in. No windows. The plaster on the walls was as grey and loose as scurf and their shadows were like giants'.

"How many of you are there?"

"Three," Liam said. "Two besides me." He found himself reaching for the bottle again; it was a third full. "Can I?"

"Go ahead. There's more."

The glow was spreading. "How much more?"

"Another bottle."

"And what's in there?" A cardboard box beside the table.

"Cigarettes, mainly."

"No food?"

"Not much."

"It's food I'm wanting. And some of the whiskey." He paused, watching their reaction. "Not for myself. For Kenny . . . he's the one of mine who's ill, badly ill."

The older man moved restlessly. As if to distract Liam he said: "You ought to be on watch, Tim." He spoke in a surly fashion. "It's lunacy for both of us to be in here."

"I've done my turn."

"I'm to go?—is that it?"

"You took the words off my tongue."

"Very well."

The man holstered his revolver and wrapped a scarf about his neck: he had a drinker's face, fleshy and suffused. He took a passing swig from the bottle, then went cautiously out, shutting the two doors quietly after him. It was almost impossible to believe that danger and darkness and death were only yards away.

"You're calm," Liam said with envy. "You're both very calm." And lucky, he thought; Jesus, yes.

"The whiskey helps."

"I meant what I said. There's one of mine needs it."

"That's for Sean to decide." He was good-looking, with a boy's eyes and a soft blond bristle on his chin. "You'll have to ask him."

"What's the food?"

"Corned beef."

"I don't want much. It's not for me or the girl. We can last a while yet, but Kenny won't." Liam stared wolfishly at the cardboard box. "We're exposed where we are. It isn't shut in like here. We're in the old hotel, first floor up, overlooking the Green, and the way Rogers spoke I never thought it would be for more than a few hours." He couldn't stop himself talking. "Every time their patrols—"

"Cigarette?"

Liam fumbled one from the crumpled yellow pack and lit it from the candle. When he inhaled the room seemed to waver.

"What's this about a girl?"

"She's with me."

"Since when?"

"Since Hafferty's."

A jet of smoke deflected off the table. "Lucky you."

"She's a headache. Wild." Liam shivered, thawing out. Then he lifted the bottle, holding what he took into his mouth and letting it trickle slowly down his throat. "She almost did for us today. About to turn sniper she was, suddenly, without thought of the consequences. Imagine it. I barely stopped her in time."

"She can shoot, can she?"

"Shoot? I'll say she can. Shoot, argue . . . and the devil knows what." The smoke curdled in the candlelight. "She's a headache, I tell you. I've never known the like. You'd hardly think it to look at her, but she's tough. I didn't come searching on her account."

"How old's this girl?"

"Your age." Liam shrugged, seduced by the whiskey and the warmth and the miracle of allies. "She's been all for pulling out of where we've landed ourselves." He drew on the cigarette, Kenny in the muzziness of his thoughts. With a renewed sense of urgency he said: "What can you spare? Apart from the hard stuff and the meat, what is there?"

"Candles, that's all."

Liam crouched by the box and flipped the lid open. There

were three battered cans of corned beef. He took hold of one and straightened up.

"Drop it."

"Surely to God—"

"Drop it," the one called Tim repeated, jerking the shotgun. Then, as if on the spur of the moment: "If you want it that bad, I'll strike a bargain with you." His lips curled with a sudden show of desperation all his own.

"What kind of bargain?"

"Bring the girl over and it's yours."

"You're joking."

"Not that I'm aware."

"Clodagh?" Liam said stupidly. "Here?"

"That's right. Take it or leave it. Get her here and the can's yours." The flame-bud blinked, weeping grease. "We've another exit, at the back. We can always pull out if it comes to the last straw. I tell you, you'll be doing her a favour."

"Look, I've got a sick man, a starving, semi-delirious—"

"D'you think we haven't been through the mill ourselves? There were five in this squad until three days ago."

"I'm not asking on my own account."

An explosion thudded in the distance. Like a bribe the bottle was thrust his way. Liam hesitated, then drank quickly, promising himself it was for the last time.

"You said to ask Sean about what I could have."

"He's no part of this."

"You said it was for him to decide."

"Don't harp on what I said. I'm talking about my own share of what's left."

"There's still Sean's."

"He'll no more separate himself from what belongs to

him than fly. He lost his brother raiding for it. So who's this Kenny of yours—or anyone—after that?" A shake of the head. "You'll be wasting your time with him."

"And with you?"

"With me you've got an offer."

Liam licked his cracked lips. There was a seashell sound inside his skull, like surf. He leaned clumsily against the table.

"Suppose the girl won't come?"

"She'd be a fool not to." Tim paused, the randy, red-eyed part of him all but masked over. "For instance, when did she last eat? Or drink, except for water." He hadn't missed much. "If she's so keen on quitting, now's her chance. Get her here and the beef's yours."

Liam couldn't hold his gaze. He glanced down, senses dulled, Clodagh and Kenny competing for his loyalty. Everything seemed to be pulsing in and out of focus.

"Listen—" he tried.

"She'll be better off here."

"If Kenny could move—"

"He can't though, can he?"

God, how quick he was. Liam made an enormous effort and managed to isolate Kenny, thinking only of him. "I'll need more than just the corned beef." All at once it had come to this; he was haggling. As if deranged he listened to the market tone of his own voice. "I want what's in the bottle as well."

"There's still a quarter left of that."

"You've got another bottle in the box, untouched. For the love of Christ," he said thickly, "this is life or death."

"Don't priest-talk me."

"I want what's in the bottle. *And* the can."

"On delivery."

Long seconds passed. Liam swayed, empty and desperate and tempted beyond recall. Outside of here there was nothing. A length of curtain and a freezing wilderness— that and nothing else, nothing else anywhere. All too well he knew it.

"She'll be no use to you." He glared at the young, ruthless face as though it were an enemy's. "She's not the kind you're thinking."

"I'll be the judge of that."

Liam snorted. As fast as thought a succession of cameos of Kenny released a fresh flood of despair. He started for the door, dismayed at himself, seeking refuge and justification in everything he remembered of Clodagh's fierce and rebellious self-sufficiency.

"What's got into you?" Tim said. "Ten minutes ago you were all for having the girl out of your way."

Sean shuffled in the darkness beyond the second door. "Tim?"

"It's me," Liam breathed back.

"What's he let you have?"

"Don't sound so concerned," Liam said bitterly. "Nothing that belongs to you. Nothing even of what he claims for himself unless I bring him what he wants."

No interest, no curiosity.

"We've a girl in my squad." The whisper rustled around the walls. "In exchange I get a can of meat and a quarter of a bottle of whiskey." He paused expectantly, misled by the hurt and shame of what he felt.

"You're getting it cheap. One of ours was gunned down and left dying in the gutter."

"What's that to do with here and now?"

"I've struck no bargain." The leaden voice retained its indifference. "I'm not interested in any girl."

"Help me then. I'm hardly asking the earth. All I need—"

"And I'm not crossing him in there, if that's what you're thinking. Not in a blue moon."

Sudden hatred released Liam from where he stood and drove him viciously toward the window. Compassion was a word, comradeship a word.

"Easy," Sean hissed, alarmed. "And watch out for the searchlight."

Liam heaved himself over into the basement area and felt his way up the stone steps. The cold had been lying in wait for him and everywhere was deadly still and dangerous. He crouched on the top step, letting his eyes adjust. The searchlight was directed nowhere near, but he delayed for perhaps a minute before moving a muscle, the whiskey making him seem top-heavy. Then he went, crouching, a shadow among shadows, the frost as crisp as grit.

It took him all of half an hour to get back as far as the hotel. The curtain he retrieved within ten or fifteen yards; wrapped in a roll around his shoulders it didn't impede him. He worked his way between the solid dunes of rubble and across the loose litter of smashed stretches of pavement, going sideways, facing outwards, past where the dead man was, past all the places where others might be hidden, dead or alive. No patrol came near. Once, for a few seconds, the searchlight pinned him motionless and he watched with dread as his breath rose like mist into the beam, but he was spared the sickening heart-in-mouth tensions of the outward trip.

A few shots crackled like static to the north as he made the last few yards up to the bathroom-level and squeezed carefully over the crest of the parapet. At first he could see nothing, but he could hear Kenny and it was awful to hear; worse.

"I watched you," Clodagh said, soft as a ghost and nearer than he realized. "I've been on the look-out and glimpsed you at the last."

"Has he coughed?"

"He seems to have gone past that. . . . Did you manage something?"

"Here."

Liam pulled the length of curtain from his shoulders and their hands touched as they made the exchange.

"Velvet, is it?"

"Curtaining."

"Anything else?" He heard her flip the material over Kenny.

"Nothing on me."

"He's desperate." Then, with disbelief: "You've been drinking."

"True."

"Whiskey."

"Right," he said. "Now listen to this. I've found a place where it's better. Sixty, seventy yards—that sort of thing, though it seems more. A basement, with a cellar and a back way."

"How in the name—?"

"I slipped. Fell in. Someone had a gun to my head as quick as blinking."

"God," she said. "Who's there?"

"Two men." He hesitated fractionally. "And they've food with them—corned beef—as well as whiskey. Not much of either, but some. And they're in the cellar and can burn a candle and it isn't icy like here."

"Kenny's beyond moving. Listen to him. Even a stone's-throw's too far for him now."

"A few sips might pick him up, just sufficient to—"

"Sips of what?"

"I'm going back for it."

"Again? ... Back there? ... You're muddling me," she said slowly. "Couldn't you have brought it now and saved the risk?"

"I'm going for it," he repeated, "and I want you to come."

"Me?"

"That's why I'm here."

"Who says I want to go?"

"It's the best thing."

"What if I refuse?"

"You've too much sense to refuse."

"But Kenny. . . ." Her voice sounded brittle, as if her teeth were clamped against the cold.

"There's no point in everyone staying until Kenny's capable of shifting. Three of us would never be able to make the trip at the same time." He despised his own plausibility. "Two of us together will be bad enough; three impossible. I'll take you to where the others are, then turn about. They've promised me all they can spare." The words jarred. He shut his mind against the recollection of the shiny hunger in the eyes awaiting her. "Kenny won't be left alone for long."

"He's awful bad, Liam."

She had never used his name before. "What d'you expect?" he retorted, sharper than he realized. "I missed the boat for him, didn't I? Haven't you kept on reminding me?"

"I thought we were alone, that's why. Us and no one else."

"Well, we aren't. And I'm told there's others besides the two I found."

"Where?"

"I wish to God I knew."

"Haven't you been lucky enough?"

He held his tongue, trapped by memory and imagination. Kenny sobbed as he breathed, lungs rasping like a file on wood.

"What time is it?"

"One-ish," Liam said without checking.

Clodagh was on her haunches, just visible to him now. "I never thought we'd split."

"Well, we've got to, and that's that." He wasn't allowing her a moment; or himself. "Get your rifle."

"It's here."

"And ammo?"

"Yes."

"Come on, then. And stay with me—right on my heels."

Even then she hesitated, just when he thought she was about to follow, and in the state of mind that was his it seemed as if her words were chosen to touch his conscience on the raw.

"Liam—"

"What?"

"I could have waited. You should have brought the stuff for Kenny first."

They went as quiet as thieves, up and over and down,

Liam experienced in where to make for and where to avoid, lessons learned. The searchlight gave them few qualms, the beam mainly concentrated on the side streets, only occasionally swivelling their way. In the darkness on the reverse slopes of the rubble-heaps their worst danger was noise—something struck, something disturbed; there was flotsam in all directions. And where there was a faint sheen of reflected light and they could pick their way with more precision, then the feeling of exposure was intense and their nerves were wire-taut, quivering. "Down!" Liam jerked once, grabbing at Clodagh to force her flat, and they pressed behind the crashed remains of a lamp-post, eyes wide, ears straining, only to realize it was a false alarm.

Wispy feathers of purplish light stroked the sky to the east of the Green. Voices reached them from the other end and a car pulled in behind where the gutted tram was. Footsteps sounded, though no one showed. Liam kept signalling, indicating the next move, lips moving soundlessly —"Crawl... Mind this... Go round...." The rifle hampered Clodagh and when she dragged herself close to the ground the slung bandoliers got in her way; several times he winced, catching his breath, reliving the brief and self-same rise and fall of alarm as metal scraped on stone.

"Keep in, keep in...." He pointed, nearing the basement. As she crawled alongside the light went careering overhead and he vividly remembered being in Hafferty's yard, torches flicking this way and that, and bending towards her in dawning astonishment—"You're a woman, aren't you?" The tunic and the trousers and the cropped hair weren't much of a disguise, not even in the dark. And now he glimpsed her face again and saw how unutterably strained and exhausted she was.

"This is it." The gouged-out, three-storeyed remains reared above them. He risked a soft command. "Follow me down."

At the bottom, in the narrow area, he waited for her to come. And another waited, too—inside the gaping square of the window; Liam could feel a presence.

"You've brought her, then." It was Sean.

"There's a sill," Liam said to Clodagh. "You can step through. After that he'll show you."

"Aren't you coming?" she asked.

"Not now." In a low voice that didn't seem like his own he said to Sean: "I want the can and the rest of the bottle."

"I have them here."

He fumbled for them; took them. "Goodbye now," he said into the blackness where Clodagh had gone, on the brink of saying more and unable to; feeling old suddenly, wretched, his heart like stone.

He didn't wait. He went up the steps to ground level, pocketing the squat can, the bottle jammed underarm. As he crouched, ready to crawl away, he thought he heard a murmured exchange below, but he wasn't sure. Two emotions were overlapping as he started furtively on the return journey. The hollow-hungry mask of her drawn, wide-eyed expression kept pace with him, and with a kind of heartbreak he knew how easy it had been to entice her.

The glow of the whiskey was already fading: the cold was eating through again, filling his mind and body. He moved on hands and knees, shielding the precious bottle. A patrol nosed by and he pressed into a dip of broken stone, petrified; for a while the searchlight appeared to hunt him, cat and mouse. There were moments when time seemed to lose its shape as fear slid its tentacles around his guts. Yet he survived, the bottle too. Weak and shaking he reached the front of the hotel and wormed his way over the cone of rubble up to the bathroom, Kenny's bubbling, sing-song dirge audible even before Liam rolled in over the parapet.

Like a blind man he felt his way to Kenny's side, assailed by loneliness and a sense of deprivation such as he had experienced only once before. He knelt and lifted Kenny's head with one hand and tilted the slopping bottle with the other.

"Drink," he said quietly. "Try and get some of this into you."

4

THE FLAME OF the candle fluttered in the used air as the cellar door was opened. In an instant of heightened awareness Clodagh took in the shotgun on the table and the man sitting in the chair and the mattress and the stained walls and the cardboard box; and heard the door shut behind her and realized the other man had gone; and felt the small rise in temperature like balm.

"So he got you here all right."

She nodded, nostrils flared, and he studied her intently, very alert as he rose to his feet. Her left hand was streaked with blood.

"You're cut, did you know?"

"Glass." She put the hand to her mouth and sucked the base of the thumb, the wound brilliant against the pallor of her skin.

"How d'you like this place? A real snug, eh? Home from home."

"It's all right."

"Better than where you came from?"

"It's all right," she said.

"You're well out of that. In the old hotel, wasn't it?" He spotted the caution in her eyes: everything showed in the eyes, always. "Don't worry—he told us where you were."

"Why ask me, then?"

He grinned, riding it. "I heard, too, that you're extra special with a gun."

"I wouldn't have said so."

"Smoke?"

"I don't." She laid the rifle on the table and stripped off the bandoliers.

"A drop of whiskey?"

She nodded, arms wrapped across herself, lower lip trembling, rivers of exhaustion leaden and deep within her.

"Clodagh, isn't it?"

"If that's what you were told."

"Only that," he said. "No more."

He opened the lid of the box and lifted out a full bottle, then drew the cork.

"It's better not to have names," she said.

"Why's that?"

"In case you're caught. You can't tell what you haven't heard."

He passed her the bottle. "What about him who brought you?"

"What about him?"

"Did you never hear his name? Not once?"

"I did, yes."

"And the other fellow's, the one that's sick?"

"Yes."

"Well, then." He grinned again. "I'm Tim Carroll. And Sean O'Malley's outside the door."

Two-handed she raised the bottle to her lips and drank, then gasped, bending over. A shudder ran through her from head to toe.

"Good?"

She nodded, eyes closed, cheeks sucked in. When she opened her eyes they were swimming.

"Famished, are you? Corned beef is all we've got, and not much of that." His voice was thicker than Liam's; more in the throat. "We're depleted, you could say."

He reached down into the box, took out a can and began to peel it open with the key. She stared as if mesmerized while he pulled with his fingers at the exposed chunk of compressed and mottled meat, breaking some off.

"How's that?"

She stuffed it ravenously into her mouth, chewed and swallowed, he on one side of the table, she on the other. Then she drank from the bottle a second time, silver globules of air gurgling through the amber fluid.

"Where's this back way out?"

"Left past the door. A coal chute. You're slim enough to wriggle through, if and when it comes to that." He paused very slightly. "You're just the right shape in every way."

He caught her flashing glance, but failed to hold it beyond a moment, unable to decipher its message.

"More of this?"

He offered another greasy wedge of corned beef. She took it from him without a word and he watched her eat, tense as he did so, aware of her own tension and her own watchfulness. Suddenly she stiffened: a faint but steady tapping could be heard.

"What's that?"

"Someone in the same boat as ourselves." He shrugged. "At first we thought it might be a trick—banging on a bit of gas pipe somewhere and seeing if there's any response. But not after two nights and a day." The tapping vibrated softly in the cellar ceiling. "No one's got the patience to pretend that long."

Casually he picked up the rifle and the shotgun and stood them against the far wall. Then he covered over what remained of the meat with the peeled-off top of the can and put it back in the box, doing this with a certain deliberateness. Then he grinned once more, confident and slightly leering.

"Out of sight, out of mind."

"For you, maybe. You've had it soft."

"*We* have?"

"From the look of it."

"There were five of us at the start. If you'd been with us—"

"It's here I'm talking about."

"Don't tell me you're complaining."

She sucked at her thumb and made no reply. The tapping had stopped. There was gunfire now and she stood with her head a little to one side, translating the sound; below ground level it was different, more remote, lacking the prickling sense of danger.

"Don't you ever go outside?" she asked suddenly. "Or does the other one like all the dark and freezing cold?"

"We each do our share."

He stared at her across the candlelight, and with something like contempt she stared back, unease mingled with it.

There were faces like his to be found at home—in the dance-hall at weekends and on the corners any evening. And there were girls who'd abandoned home because of them, implausible excuses left behind—the 'too-soon-loved' her father used to say they were. The unease she felt increased her tension, and when he began to move around the table she was jolted instinctively into looking to where he'd placed the Lee-Enfield.

He nodded at the bottle. "D'you want another swallow?"

"Not now."

"It's marvellous heating. And there's more to spare of it than there is the corned beef."

"No."

"Take a rest then." He was watching a throbbing in her throat. "There's a mattress going to waste if you don't."

"I'm fine where I am."

"Standing?"

She perched herself on the table, one foot touching the stone floor. "Here," she said.

"That's no place to be. Not sat up there like a bird."

"I like it."

After all the vengeful fighting and the sights and sounds of death and mutilation she had thought that she was done with being afraid. But she was wrong; suddenly and without warning she was gusted toward fear by his strangeness and the yellow-lit look of him and her own stubborn mania about human purity and physical defilement and disgrace— all this and more compressed into the space of seconds and revealed in her face.

"Clodagh."

"What d'you want?"

He took another step, angered by her innocence, the anger

showing in blue and bloodshot eyes. Wild, the fellow who'd brought her had said. Well, then.

"Touch me and I'll kill you."

"You don't know what you're saying."

"I swear it." She edged away, thinking with desperation of Liam, scared of the lovelessness that would go with the pain. "Lay hands on—"

He made a grab, but she eluded him, managing to keep the table in between.

"You don't kid me," he said confidently, "so don't try. You haven't a hope."

He feinted, disguising the direction he was coming from, but she wasn't deceived. She darted behind the chair, a cry forming but choked down. The guns were out of reach. He came after her, cat-like on his toes, and she flung the chair at him. In three strides she reached the door and wrenched it open and went blundering into the narrow corridor that led to the chute, going anywhere, anywhere to get away, tripping, falling, floorboards breaking underfoot.

And not escaping.

He caught up with her and wrestled her to a standstill, pulling her close, his blond bristle against her face.

"See?" he said, breathing hard. "Where would you have gone to, anyway?"

She spat at him blindly, kicking and twisting.

"Not out into the Green, surely?" He was triumphant. "Don't tell me you've got friends out there."

The other door had opened and shut. "What's happening, for Christ's sake?"—Sean.

"Nothing that concerns you."

"The din concerns me."

70

"You won't hear it again."

Clodagh was lifted from behind, arms pinioned to her sides. Sean followed them into the cellar-room, and for a brief moment she thought he was about to intervene. Indignation hardened the surly set of his face, but it wasn't until the last that she realized he was looking beyond her. He went accusingly to the bottle on the table and picked it up.

"You haven't wasted time."

"All in a good cause." The chuckle was alongside her right ear.

"Help me." Her voice cracked. "Don't let him."

Sean took a double swig of whiskey. His indifference seemed to liquidize her stomach and she pleaded with him, half-throttled, an arm across her throat.

"You're in command. Tell him to stop. *Order* him . . . Jesus, isn't this your squad?"

Sean set the bottle down. "No, it isn't." He wouldn't look at her. He wanted no part of it. He turned his back and went out, and the voice by her ear said with satisfaction: "There, you see?"

She cried, without a sound. No moans, no sobs, not using tears as a weapon but with every scrap of her courage gone and in need of sanctuary. The one who held her could feel her shaking as he pulled her round to face him. And she could see her fear mirrored in the dark glossy pupils of his eyes.

When, on the mattress, she arched her back and called out, riven, scalding, he threatened her. "Stop it," he told her fiercely, pressing down, not raising his voice. "Shut up." Even then.

Before and after, with her head turned sideways, she stared woodenly at the guns propped against the wall. Before, while he was dragging at her clothing or as he explored her with his hands she was in terror of his strength, his power. "What are you afraid of, eh?" He said it several times. "Come on, now." He was only really savage at the last. He was animal-crude and eager until then, sliding his hands, chasing her mouth with his, and she flinched endlessly from the feel of him, face averted, eyes closed, body stiff and unresponsive.

"Come on now," he kept breathing. "Christ above."

And afterwards, as the terror went out of her until it was only fear again, fear and disgust and shock, he didn't discard her as most would have done but continued to hold her in the crook of his arm, as if to keep her from going to the guns. "Was it so bad?" Callous, lighting a cigarette and blowing smoke and being caustic. "Like a plank, you were."

Within her mind she fled from him, seeking refuge where she had once belonged, gazing as if in a dream at the sight of fuchsia abounding in autumn hedges along the lanes, the wind-broken blossoms lying as bright as fresh blood, and elsewhere bracken dead and brown like blood that had dried, and the look of deserted barricades about the ragged stone walls, and all the trees grown with a permanent lean from the south-west, and a white cottage and blue water and slate-grey hills, and turf piled at the roadside and long black trenches cut in the bog.

"You asked for it, didn't you?—going to Hafferty's yard and all."

There was no escape. Her body burned from him, but the past culminated in anguish and hatred of its own. The obscenity of her father's death had led her to Hafferty's, and time and chance and Liam Gallagher had brought her in turn to where she was now.

She fought hysteria down. At all costs she must avoid hysteria. The wick sparked in the candle-flame and everywhere the shadows jumped, bent round the walls. She stared at the flame, brutally humiliated and wishing to God himself that she had never left Liam's side, thinking of his sad drawn face and worn and wrinkled clothes with immense and sudden longing. "Dreaming, girl?" her father used to tease. "Romancing, are you, in that head of yours?" Not any more.

Tears once more blurred her vision. She would have prayed but she had lost the taste for prayer. She clenched hands and jaws and glanced again at the rifle that was hers and listened to the small noises and the stone-dead silence that came from the ruins above their heads.

All her life this mildewed place would haunt her, always, whatever happened. And the shame.

"Are you still with that notion of killing me?" He chuckled, a veneer. "Well, are you?"

She didn't answer.

"Plenty of others would have done what I did. Beats me why nobody's done it to you before, if you ask me. Those two you were with, for instance."

"They're . . . not pigs."

"So you've a tongue after all?" He was buttoning himself. "I always say that so long as both parties have tongues in their heads there's no reason why they shouldn't part friends. And haven't we an enemy in common?"

"I pick and choose my own."

"They happen to be mine as well."

73

"Not all," she flashed, and the bite in her voice was savage.

He winced theatrically. "No one's ever what they seem."

"You flatter yourself."

In a low voice she then said; "They're coming here. Just as soon as Kenny's able to be shifted."

"Who gave you that idea?"

"Liam."

A long thin ribbon of smoke rose from his cigarette. "News to me."

"They're coming," she insisted.

"What's that meant to do?—give me a fright?"

He flicked the cigarette-butt across the cellar and heaved himself into a sitting position. Tiny wedges of white muck were in the corners of his eyes. He leaned on an elbow, still angered by her innocence yet not in the same way. "What harm's been done? You're a big girl now." He grinned maliciously and she bit at his hand, nipping flesh, and he yelped.

"Bitch."

He swore at her, then rose and drank from the bottle, baring his teeth as the stuff went down. From the table he looked at her with a kind of jeering resentment.

"Is that what he palmed you off with?—that he was joining you?"

"As soon as Kenny's up to it."

"And you believed him?"

"We'd have waited and come together if he'd thought that three could risk it at once."

He smirked. "How long have you been playing soldiers with the boys?"

She fingered her bruised mouth, repugnance and grief

and hatred maturing, becoming one. "Liam's not your kind."

"It takes all sorts to make a world—even a new one."

"When Liam says a thing—"

"I thought you didn't bandy names about." He paused, tormenting her. The line of his mouth had hardened. "Mr. Halo—why not call him that?"

He moistened his lips, one after the other. Under her tunic, between firm small-nippled breasts, a metal cross hung on a thin chain, and the moment his eager fingers had touched it he knew that part of her fear was of what she thought evil to be. All too often for him a woman's body went part-and-parcel with a child's mind, and all too often it was the child who afterwards surveyed the grubby rags of intimacy and wept and called him a lecher. Time and again he'd been washed into a mist as they prayed, hailing Mary, shaming and killing him with their consciences.

"Mr. Halo now," he said again. "Mr. Knight-in-shining-armour."

The tapping started up, different from before, more urgent, like a warning. A frown creased his forehead. He gazed at Clodagh, lust gone from him, strain filling the void it had left—the days-long strain of clinging to the hems of hope.

"If the other fellow's so bad, and considering what it's like out there, how d'you suppose your Mr. Halo's going to get him here at all?"

She tossed her head, regretting being drawn, having spoken. She tried to escape him again, no longer fleeing for solace to the poignancies of the past but focussing on Liam and short hours ago, recalling glimpses of him as the searchlight came swinging round, unable to find expression for her feelings yet knowing that what she identified was truly indispensable, filling a desolation.

"You want the best of everything, don't you?"

Despite herself she met his stare, unable to obliterate the feel of him, the sound of him, remembering the beasts in the field.

"Women and children first—all that."

"No."

"And then you expect a tunic with buttons on to camouflage you out of sight. Trousers, short hair . . . Christ alive. You're on a cloud, girl. The world isn't the way you seem to think. Shall I tell you something?"

Her look seemed to enrage him. He jabbed a finger at her.

"Shall I tell you one more fact of life that's clearly passed you over?"

The tapping was rising to a crescendo, like nails being driven home.

"When Mr. Halo man came blundering into here, desperate on the other fellow's behalf—"

He got no further. The door was flung open. Sean was there, revolver drawn, gesturing.

"Quick," he said, like a kick in the brain. "Up and out. They're beginning a search."

They went for the guns, grabbing at bandoliers and shrugging them on, the flame shaking as they passed it by. The bottle toppled and broke, whiskey spilling down.

"How close?"

"Next door."

They cannoned into one another. Tim scrabbled in the cardboard box, scattering cigarettes, burrowing deeper.

"Leave that!"

"Half a mo—"

He pulled out a can of meat, dropped it, swore, hesitated, abandoned it.

"Come *on!*"

All this in seconds. Sean blew out the candles as they crushed through the door, Clodagh sandwiched between the two of them. Outside, at ground level, someone was bawling: "Anyone gone into this one? . . . Right, Sergeant —see to it."

The hoarse command was amplified by the emptiness of the front room. A moment later footsteps thudded along the brink of the basement area.

Sean bundled Clodagh from behind, pushing her into the dark where she had earlier tried to flee. They were clipping each others' heels, stealth impossible, frantic in the hope that a grenade wouldn't be a preliminary. After a few stumbling paces the broken floorboards ended and they were on a firm surface, cement, something loose and chunky piled to the sides. Coal; Clodagh could smell it. She followed Tim, clutching at his belt, briefly severed in her mind from what he was, everything swamped by the sound of others coming.

Suddenly he stopped and reached up, dragging himself on to a ledge. There was a clank above their heads and a crescent of sky appeared, then a full round circle as he shifted a manhole cover. He shoved his shotgun through and went after it, legs like a swimmer's, Clodagh on the ledge and Sean already urging her to go, agitated, torchlight probing only a couple of rooms behind, around two corners.

"Now! . . . Now!"

He gave her a heave. Above the ledge the wall was angled. She got head and shoulders into the hole. Tim was waiting for her, waiting for them both, hauling them out like ferrets, one by one. They clamped the cover back on and dragged a heavy chunk of masonry across—Sean's idea, sealing off the possibility of direct pursuit.

Close in to a wall they paused, gathered together, alarm pulsing in their ears. Nothing moved. Clodagh peered to left and right, straining her eyes, ravages everywhere, the cold as icy as before. Shouting was still coming from the front of the houses, and with a pang she thought of Kenny and Liam, scared for them, wondering if they were up to the moving yet, willing it so. She belonged with them.

"What made them search?" Sean whispered, not to her. "It makes no sense this late in the—"

"The tapping, was it?"

"You think so?"

"What else?" Tim answered. "Unless Rogers has started at last."

A flash lit the sky like a great falling sheet of green glass, giving them a fleeting glimpse of ruin. They were in a sort of alley between a maze of back gardens and tumble-down outbuildings. The glitter of frost was on everything—aiding vision, hinting at the hazards that lay between them and the river: what they could vaguely see was only a beginning.

"Come on."

Tim led, Sean next, Clodagh last. The men were blowing hard. She moved stiffly in their wake, shock and outrage dulled to a cancerous ache by the tingling renewal of danger. The firing was heavier than for days, and it seemed to have spread along an arc to the north of them. Undeniably it was nearer. Half-left, at roof-level, something burst like a thunder-clap, spattering a shower of burning rain; ahead, no more perhaps than a couple of blocks away, a machine-gun was hammering out its screeching message. But at first, for them, it was like the eye of a storm; they made fifty yards through the no-man's-land in which they found themselves, immune, the sobbing whine of ricochets no worse than old warnings. It was only when they reached the alley's end between walls of corrugated iron sheeting that progress came to an abrupt halt.

They had travelled in small rushes, jinking from point to point, scarcely pausing. Now they piled into one another, confronted by the width of a street; and there were troops in it. They could hear the shuffling of them and see their cigarettes—a platoon maybe, massed near the corner where the street joined another, behind cover, waiting.

"Walk," Tim breathed over his shoulder. "Make for the gap by the garage. Walk it—straight over. Quiet as a mouse, now."

He sounded cool enough. He signalled to Clodagh. It was all of thirty paces, and after the first half-dozen every nerve in her body was screaming at her to run. She walked as if she were blindfold on a wire without a net, searching with her feet. It seemed impossible that nobody would notice her; one turned head and she was surely done for. Every second of the way she was flinching expectantly from a challenge that never came. She crept in beside the garage and watched the others, what she felt for them suspended, sharing each step, each unbreathing pause, each awful hesitancy.

She shivered with relief as they joined her, the irony bitter and inescapable. Moments too late to trap them a flare throbbed a silver light into the street and they saw the soldiers clearly and the rows of small drab broken and abandoned houses. On a word the soldiers debouched into the main street and almost immediately a sniper loosed off. The night was beginning to crackle everywhere and some of it was close.

"Come on"—Tim again.

In a fever she thought of Liam and the faith he'd had in Rogers. She was wrong and he was right; the promised attack was on its way in. This was it, gathering momentum. It had to be. Tapping hadn't caused that search along the Green. It was Rogers, regrouped and fighting back, and Liam was both justified and endangered.

God, she asked, see him out of there—and safe.

"D'you reckon we'll be counter-attacking by the morning?"—Kenny's question wouldn't leave her alone as she moved with the other two. How she'd gone at Liam, on and on.

They were past the garage and into another labyrinth of urban squalor—sheds and bits of fencing and places boarded over, empty buildings without doors, gutted workshops, names and signs belonging to other days. They moved in a crisp white frosty darkness, chimneys and jagged shapes against the sky, and the sky was all the time exploding yellow and pink and orange.

"How far to the river?" Sean panted, in a sweat.

"Which way's more like it."

Not so cool now. They retreated from a cul-de-sac and tried another dog-leg route. Pain jarred through Clodagh's frame. Slogans on the walls; elsewhere the stench of drains. They were fired on as they crossed to a gap by a mews, the air plucked inches overhead—*zip-zip-zip*. Their surroundings crowded in, containing them, confusing them. Sometimes they were stabbed with brightness as they moved, and sometimes they huddled as still as stone with the night pumping behind their eyes. Minute by minute there was less room for manoeuvre.

They scrambled over a low roof, dropped into a yard, emerged into a second street beside a pebbledashed pub. The sign was punched through with bullet-holes and the shutters were up like everywhere else. Firing was heavy and continuous now, scarcely a bomb's-throw away, yet the street itself was empty, littered with debris from the remains of a hasty barricade. Tim crossed and turned left and the instant he did so Clodagh knew he'd made a mistake.

"Where in God's name's he going?"

Sean faltered. "What's wrong?"

"It's the other way. The river's—"

Her throat contracted. A Whippet armoured car had appeared at the end of the street. With terrifying abruptness headlamps were beamed full on, trapping Tim in an oval splash against the wall.

Only him.

There was a kind of slow-motion inevitability as he turned on heel and toe, firing blindly from the hip in an impotent gesture of defiance. But the gunner in the turret was quicker, far quicker, and more accurate. His target crumpled as if strings had been cut, face contorted and upturned. Vividly Clodagh saw where the blood was, and wondered in a flash and without madness how so smashed and limp a body could ever have been so violent.

Beyond that she felt nothing. Nothing.

"Run," Sean was yelling. "For Christ's sake—"

5

THE HEADLIGHTS couldn't follow them both. For a quivering second they fell on Sean, then abandoned him for Clodagh, lost her in turn and jerked uncertainly elsewhere, the air demented as the machine-gun yapped, dust erupting where the bullets smashed, orders and the crash of gears echoing between the houses.

The only cover was the breached barricade—a handcart, tar drums, household wreckage; it helped to reprieve them, though not for long. Pursuit was immediate, the armoured car accelerating. The street emptied into a concrete playground with slides and swings and turntables. A high wall ringed the area round, but there was nowhere else to go. They separated, swerving left and right. Clodagh was staggering, her legs like lead. She scrambled behind a seesaw, shaking so much she couldn't steady herself, hiding like a child but spent as no child ever was, gasping, threads of spittle on her cheeks.

The armoured car screeched to a standstill. Sean must have gone shouldering into the swings; the chains were twitching in the headlights. Four men came with a clatter out of the street, rifles at the ready, and positioned themselves by the end house—the tam-o'-shanters branded them; Auxiliaries.

The night was exploding everywhere but here. Here it was stealthy and still, just an engine ticking over and a cat mewing on the near wall, just Sean and herself and the car and the four men. The whole of her life had narrowed down to here and now. And no way out, not a hope.

In low gear the armoured car began to turn, wheeling clockwise on full lock. She could have shot the turret-gunner dead or picked off any of the men crouched by the house; it would have been simple. Yet her thumb stayed on the safety-catch. For the first time since they'd sheared her hair something more than murder was in her heart. She was beaten, trapped, at bay; but trembling within her exhaustion was a yearning to survive.

Panting, she watched the headlights slew through ninety degrees. A climbing-frame, the car's tracks scrawled on the carpet of frost, the high enclosing wall.

"They're here somewhere," a voice said. "No bloody doubt. Two of 'em."

The lights moved closer, pausing where Sean's scarf lay twisted on the ground. The cat mewed once again, fear in the sound. She wanted to live. Oh Jesus, she wanted to live—not just for living's sake, not just for herself, not suddenly out of cowardliness or overwhelmed by mercy or forgiveness or restraint. More to it than that, frailty a part of it, exhaustion, shock, defilement, tears.

And Liam.

A shot made her stiffen. Sean darted from behind the children's slide, revolver in hand, side-stepping frantically as the headlights followed. He must have known it was futile. There were shouts from where the men were by the house, like the cries back home when the rabbits were flushed out of the crops and the guns picked them off. Then another shot cracked like a whip and Sean went sprawling as though he'd met a tripwire.

"That's one of 'em."

Now it was coming. The turret-gunner was etched solid against the sky, easy, but Clodagh laid the rifle down. As the armoured car nosed round and the leading edge of the lights reached the seesaw she was paralysed with terror, nothing like it in her life before, prayer unbidden in her mind and on her lips.

Holy Mary, mother of God, pray for us sinners now and at the hour of our death. . . .

She closed her eyes, the lights practically head-on. She was shaking uncontrollably but the paralysis had passed. If there was a chance, this was it. She raised her hands in surrender, forcing herself slowly to her feet, in dread of every life-long second and what might smash her down.

"Hold it!"

A thud, metal on metal. Nothing more. Too scared to look, too soon to hope.

Then, to her: "Keep your hands where they are!"

She did as she was told, swaying. Footsteps sounded on the concrete, approaching at the trot. She made slits of her eyes against the headlights. Two men, their bulky silhouettes rimmed with brightness. One gestured with his rifle as they closed in.

"All the way! On your toes!"

She obeyed. Hands started to hurry over her, patting, searching. Almost at once they stopped. She was gripped thumb-and-finger by the chin and her head turned sideways.

"Stone the crows, Jack."

"What's up?"

"You'll never believe what's here. Not in a hundred bleeding years."

She was alive, though. Relief swept her, taking her in the legs. She staggered and grabbed at the seesaw, forgetting it would tilt, sinking into a green haze as her body weighed it down. Roughly she was yanked upright.

"Wants to play games, she does."

The haze cleared, her nausea remained. The man not holding her picked up the discarded rifle.

"This all?"

She nodded.

"It 'ad better be."

He emptied the magazine, racketing the bolt back and forth, five rounds flicking out. Then he pulled the bandoliers from off her shoulders. Then he stood in front of her and ran his hands over her once more, blatantly, with a chuckle, spacing what he said.

"Surprise . . . Surprise."

She didn't move, whole areas dead in her mind.

"Get 'er over to the car."

She went without protest, one arm hooked behind her in a half-Nelson. The sky double-blinked and there was a crumbling roar, like a building coming down. Somewhere beyond the surrounding wall a machine-gun was persistently answered by rifle-fire.

"We only winged the other bastard," someone said from the armoured car. "More's the pity."

Sean was propped against the wall, the right leg of his trousers ripped and bloodstained at the thigh. One of the Auxiliaries retrieved the scarf and tossed it at him. "You'll live," he said brusquely. "Make do with that."

The headlamps were dimmed. The voice from the turret said: "How in the hell did they get round the back of us?"

"Ask 'em."

"This surly bugger's like a clam."

"Ask the girl."

"Girl?"

"Ours is a girl."

"Funny joke."

"What'll you bet?"

The others came closer, peered, whistled. Clodagh looked through them, untouched by their astonishment, unprovoked by the grinning crudity of their reaction. The more heavily built of the two had a single stripe on his greatcoat sleeves.

"All right," he said, the imported accent hard and difficult on the ear. "*You* tell us. How did you get here? . . . From which direction?"

Nerves made Clodagh toss her head.

"Which way did you come?"

She dropped her gaze. He struck her on the side of the jaw with the flat of his hand, hard, raising it ready to cuff her again.

"Remember now?"

"No," she said, revived by the blow, hate glittering in the depths of her eyes.

"Shit," the man said, "they're all the stinking same." He looked up at the turret, his breath like ectoplasm.

"What would you do?"

"Get 'em back to H.Q."

"Easier said than done."

Flames were staining the under-belly of the clouds.

"This isn't a bus, if that's what you're hoping. God Almighty. Make 'em walk."

"H.Q.'s well out of my sector."

"And mine."

"Well, then—"

"You can detach one man, can't you? From the look of 'em they'll hardly need more. I'm not wasting either my fire-power or my mobility at a time like this. . . . Let's move, driver."

The armoured car whined away in low gear. With a sour expression the lance-corporal watched it go, then turned to where Sean was.

"Get him on his feet, Page, and escort the pair of them to H.Q. And make bloody sure you've got some proof of delivery when you report back—understood?"

"Understood, Corp."

"Right, then. Get on with it." He gave Clodagh a shove. "Your boy-friend's in need of a hand."

Sean flung an arm across her shoulders as if she mattered to him; irony had no end. When the wounded leg took his weight he howled with his face to the sky. "No! . . . Christ, no!"

"Come on," the one called Page snapped. "We 'aven't got all night." He was small and ferret-featured and was carrying their weapons—the rifle slung and the revolver stuck in his webbing. "Speed it up," he urged from behind, his own rifle levelled at the hip. "You can do better than that."

As long as they were in earshot of the lance-corporal his tongue never stopped. But once they were round the first corner he relented slightly. "Rest if you want. One minute, that's all." He stayed close, though not too close, risking nothing.

Clodagh said: "How far are we going?"

"Count your lucky stars you aren't bleeding well dead, and shut your mouth. . . . Right, let's get started."

They hobbled through the havoc of the streets, thirty or forty paces without pausing. A lorry loaded with helmeted troops crunched in the other direction. Twice they passed intersections where machine-gun posts were being sand-bagged into doorways. Debris was everywhere, destruction shown to them in staccato flutters of eerie light. Fighting seemed to be growing in severity on both sides of them, as if Rogers was striking in a pincer movement.

Clodagh limped with Sean in a loveless embrace, indifferent to his pain and his cursing, her feelings measured by his own indifference when it had mattered, stunned by it still and never going to forget.

She hadn't a notion of where she was. She wasn't thinking of escape or of what came next. Survival was all—hers and Liam's. She kept telling herself that she would be able to shut her mind to everything else if only he were safe. The haggard face, the bad teeth, the bitten nails, the worn grey look of him—he wasn't much in that respect. But there was strength, and it was strength she needed, strength and tenderness and regard. She'd been conscious of them all in him at different times. And scorned them; managed without. "Goodbye"—even at the basement window his voice had been thick with concern.

So much she remembered now.

Sean yelped and stumbled, leaning on her, arm heavy around her neck. Something flashed, its dazzling intensity familiar. She raised her head and was astonished to find they were back at the Green, at the corner nearest the hotel. She had come full circle—almost. And on the way she had been destroyed, then spared and left with a longing.

"Move." As if from habit. "Sharp about it."

"Which way?"

"Straight over."

They jarred across the intervening tarmac and passed under the rime-laden branches of the plane trees, heading diagonally for the bandstand. The searchlight was aimed elsewhere, deep into a side street. Clodagh kept looking left, attention concentrated on the hotel as the angle widened, the crumbled façade very clear—the bathroom window, the rubble, everything. A dozen questions ached for an answer as they laboured into the centre of the Green, level with the bandstand and then beyond, directed with a kind of in-evitability toward the gutted tram and the baker's shop behind it where Liam had located a look-out post.

"What time is it?" she asked the Auxiliary.

"Who cares?"

"Tell me."

"Five?" he relented.

She was beside herself with exhaustion. "Where to now?"

"Just keep going."

They rounded the tram and turned a corner, where a column of soldiers waited in reserve. A back entrance to the baker's shop was flanked by two armed sentries, slapping their hands against the cold. Inside the double doors a hurricane-lamp stood at the foot of a flight of stairs which led out of a kind of lobby; the lamp was only a glimmer and it was hard to distinguish anything.

"Up," the Auxiliary said, prodding at Sean.

"I'll never—"

"*Up!*"

The air was sour with the smell of stale yeast. There was a table on the landing, another lamp, posters pinned to the walls. It was brighter here. The table was draped with a brown blanket, and the man on duty wore an improvized uniform beneath his unbuttoned greatcoat. Cropped black hair, fat blotched face—he narrowed his eyes when he saw Clodagh.

"Who's the humourist?" He fingered his nose, cigarette stuck in his mouth. The voice was cruel and lazy. "Who's decided we need an early morning laugh?"

"I'm just delivering," the Auxiliary said. "And I want a receipt."

"Receipt, nothing."

"A receipt. For these as well." He thumped the rifle and revolver on the table.

"Whose was which?"

"The girl had the rifle."

"Adeste bloody fideles." Clodagh was studied again as if she were something in a cage; then addressed, mockery in the tone. "What's a nice girl like you doing with a wicked thing like this?" The man laughed silently, then switched his gaze back to the Auxiliary. "You see? Try to be civil and what d'you get in return? Piss all."

"Sign for them, will you?"

"All right, all right." He reached for a message-pad. "Don't tell me you expect names. Names are as rare as hen's teeth. Anonymous murdering bastards, that's all we've had in here." He paused, squinting through a haze of smoke. "Who's this for?"

"My corporal."

"'Received two anonymous murdering bastards'." He read as he wrote, amused. "'Plus one stolen service rifle and one stolen service revolver, both Government property'." He added the date and signed with a scratchy flourish. "How's that?"

"Thanks." The Auxiliary turned at the top of the stairs. "The one with her's wounded, by the way."

"More fool him."

They were bundled into a room which opened off the landing. It had once been a bedroom but was now a makeshift cell, stripped bare, the single window boarded over, the faded paper showing where furniture and pictures had been positioned. The door was left wide open, so there was light enough to see.

Neither of them spoke. Without a word they chose a place to subside, Sean slumping with a groan, Clodagh settling against a wall. Gunfire shook the timbers of the building as if to remind them of the cause in which they suffered, the renewed collision of a generation's hopes. But Clodagh could only respond to the violence and yearnings within herself, and the nightmares and dreams from which they sprang.

Sean slept. He curled himself on the floor and escaped the state he was in, twitching as a dog does. She shut her eyes against the sight of him, but in vain. There was a limit to rejection, and his presence was like an asterisk which led her mind again and again to where it least wanted to go.

"Like a plank you were."

There was no warmth in the room and she trembled, not just out of weakness but from everything she knew the night had done and the uncertainties of what she didn't know. She hugged herself to her drawn-up knees, intent on the hiding-place across the Green, thinking a thousand things but thinking most of all that Kenny had been too ill for Liam ever to have got him away. The hope lost all conviction the more she gave it time. And he wouldn't have abandoned him, search or no—"How could I leave Kenny?"

So he was a prisoner like herself. Or dead. Or still there, somehow still there. . . .

Dawn showed in the cracks between the boards nailed to the window. Voices came and went on the stairs and landing. Men crossed to the doorway and stared in, swung on their heels and left, exchanged obscenities with the person on duty. And outside, in the shadowless grey of early morning, the fighting seemed to crackle and reverberate even nearer than before.

A new voice was presently to be heard on the landing— quieter than the rest, yet incisive with authority. "Yessir . . . Very good, sir"—the responses it drew were prompt and repetitive. Clodagh covered her face with her hands and drank the yeast-sour air from their cup of darkness, what remained of her strength ticking silently in her wrists.

"In there, are they?"

"Yessir."

"Anyone else?"

"No one else brought in, sir. Not yet, sir."

A chair screeched as it was moved. Footsteps approached the door and halted.

"The man's wounded," the newcomer remarked after a moment.

"Yessir."

"What's been done about it?"

"Nothing, sir."

"How long's he been here?"

"Two 'n a half hours, sir."

"Where's the first-aid post?"

"Down the street, sir."

"Then get him seen to. And quick about it."

"Yessir."

Clodagh looked up. A captain, narrow face, fair moustache, revolver holstered outside the greatcoat.... Her scalp tightened. But for Liam he would have been dead since yesterday. "I had him!" As if in an echo-chamber she remembered. "Idiot... *Idiot,* you!" She stared, dumbfounded, what seemed a lifetime between then and now.

"You've done nothing about her either, I suppose?"

"She's not wounded, sir."

"D'you think I'm blind?" The tone was scathing. "See that she's given something to drink, then have her brought in to me."

He turned and went briskly away. After a few minutes Clodagh was provided with a mug of sweetened tea. The thin-lipped individual who delivered it nudged Sean with a boot. "Look alive—you're wanted."

Sean blinked awake, pupils shrinking, alarm starting to gather as his wits resurrected. "Where—?" he began.

"Never bloody well mind about where."

He heaved himself to his feet and stumbled out, followed as close as a shadow. Clodagh didn't so much as watch him go. The tea steamed, moist on her cheeks, and she sipped at it, wary of the questions that were coming and nagged by fearful questions of her own. She felt that if she could just continue for a while with the heat going into her she would save herself from being sick.

"You can sit if you like."

She had been led across the landing to this other room with its mica-covered maps where the captain was seated at a battered desk and a window to her right gave her a view of the Green. An enormous effort was required not to turn her head in the direction of the hotel; it was visible through the trees in the sharp winter light. A cold orange sun hung low in the branches.

"You can use the chair." The captain waited, twisting a signet ring on one of his fingers. "No?" He shrugged. "It's as you wish." He seemed then to withdraw from what he was about to say. "Name?"

Some decorated verse was framed in passe-partout on the wall behind the desk.

"Your name?"

Clodagh gazed past him.

>No heart is so broken
>That God cannot mend it;
>No pain is so bitter
>That God cannot end it . . . .

"You must have a name."

"Not for giving to the likes of you."

"Please yourself."

"You can ask all you want, but you'll get nothing out of me that matters."

"Do names matter?"

"Am I a fool, do you think?"

"I shouldn't imagine so," the captain said with measured

control. His eyes were cool and determined, but he didn't look at her as if she were vermin. "What part are you from?"

"I'm not telling."

"The west, is it?"

She let him guess.

"Are there others at home like you?" He studied her with a kind of puzzled concern. "Sisters?" he said. "How many sisters have you got?"

"None."

"Brothers?"

"None."

"What does your father do?"

"My father's dead." With vicious pride she said: "He was murdered."

The captain fiddled with his signet ring.

"Murdered," Clodagh repeated.

"When?" He slipped it in, aware of what she meant. "Where?" He paused, but drew a blank. "What about your mother?"

"She died."

"I'm sorry."

"Liar."

"If you say so."

She didn't trust the pity of his glance. None of them was ever to be trusted; she learned that as she had learned the Creed.

"How did you come by what you're wearing?"

"It's mine."

"An army tunic? . . . I'm not a fool either, you know." Firing snapped like burning brushwood. "I wonder if you appreciate the seriousness of your position?" He tightened the screw. "Do you realize it's within my power to have you shot?"

Clodagh lifted her chin. "Since when was it necessary to give yourselves excuses?" With a blaze of fury she began: "I could have shot you yester—"

The word faded on her lips. The captain frowned very slightly. Otherwise he didn't move a muscle.

"Me?"

She stared back, mind in a whirl like someone found out.

"Me?" he said again. "Yesterday I was never far from where we are now."

Silence, broken by the thick-set thud of an exploding grenade.

"So where were you?"

Silence. He used these silences like a weapon.

"You've seen me before?"

"No."

"Then you're an excellent actress."

She sucked in air with a shudder.

"Or wishful thinking, was it?" The captain studied her sadly. "Do you hate so much? You can die from an overdose of hate."

He shifted position, fingering his moustache as if it bothered him. He had come to this country as the summer rusted into autumn and he couldn't understand its people. He couldn't read their minds. Always, it seemed to him, they fought as if in the knowledge that others would eventually profit from their pain and recklessness. Not themselves, and never now. It was like a tradition, a recurring dream of desperation. He had lasted three years in the trenches and knew what an enemy was and how to go about an interrogation. But never before had there been

97

a stubborn, half-starved girl in front of him. Moreover, he was sorry for her—and that was unwise, a luxury the professional in him couldn't afford.

He referred to a hand-written message on the desk. "You were captured to the south of the river in a children's playground." Somehow he made it sound like a question. "You and the man."

"Are you expecting me to deny it?"

"His name?" He was in like a flash, but she buttoned her mouth. He was prepared for as much and didn't delay. "Someone else was killed nearby."

"He wasn't with us."

"Who's lying now?"

Names were what he wanted most. Names were a starting point which led to friends, associates, districts, addresses, interceptions, arrests.

"You had nothing to do with him, I suppose?"

"No." Used and cheapened and sore from him still and yet saying "No." And him dead.

"Were you ever at a place called Hafferty's?"

"No."

"The one who was killed had it written on a piece of paper. Hafferty's." The captain varied his pace, eyes not leaving hers. "That was careless, wasn't it?"

She swayed, suddenly faint.

"Why not sit?"

She shook her head.

"When did you last eat?"

"That's my business."

"Of course, I forgot." Exasperation sharpened his tone. "You'd rather starve, wouldn't you? Rather starve, rather stand, rather freeze, rather die."

His gaze drifted clear of her. He looked impatiently across the Green. An umbrella of dark smoke hung like a backcloth behind the opposite end and the angry rattle of small-arms ebbed and flowed. Clodagh risked a glance to her right. The searchlight was being trundled away. She singled out the all-important window above the dunes of rubble. Were they there? Impossibly she hoped for a tell-tale wink of the mirror, something for herself alone. "No one else brought in, sir"—she dredged her memory for the slightest clue. Not prisoners then. And not dead, please God not dead.

"How many were at Hafferty's?" The captain nearly took her by surprise.

"Ask someone who went."

"Was Rogers present?"

"Who's Rogers?"

"How many were in your squad at the beginning?" He waited as usual, then fumbled for a cigarette, then slowly shook his head. "What brought you into this, for God's sake? You, a girl like you." She baffled and disturbed him. No girl in her right mind fought alongside men. She was young enough to be his daughter. He said: "Answer me something." He hesitated. "Unofficial."

"That's an old trick."

"Unofficial," he repeated. He was filled with a sudden desire to protect. "No names, no places. Nobody will come to any harm from what you say."

"You think I believe that?"

"I only want to know about you. Not where. Not when. Only why?"

"I don't understand."

He turned the cigarette between finger and thumb. He

looked at the cropped red hair and the pale face exhausted beyond its years and the grimy end-of-tether defiance she was still able to present, and his expression softened. He was weary of war and all that went with it.

"What did you do with yourself back home?"

She shrugged.

"What other young girls did?"

"Of course."

"Going dancing? Dressing up? . . . That kind of thing?"

"Sometimes."

"Since your mother died?"

"Sometimes."

A burst of gunfire shook the empty window-frames. Clodagh jerked a glance through the trees at the smashed hotel, isolating the place where Kenny had wheezed: "Tell me it's only a matter of time, Liam. Tell me we're here for a reason. . . ." A machine-gun began to hammer, the closest yet.

"How long ago did your mother die?"

"Twelve years."

"Who brought you up? Your father?"

She nodded.

"No one else in the house?"

"No."

"What about friends?"

She licked her lips. "We had friends."

"Your father's friends or friends of your own?"

"My father's friends were my friends too."

He moved his hands. She distressed him. A girl didn't belong at the sharp end of danger. No girl, no matter what. It was wrong that her reflexes were so conditioned that revenge was all she had been able to contemplate; revenge was the wildest kind of justice.

"Were you never in love?" he said.

She didn't answer.

"There's more to life than hating. Remember that when this is over. Get yourself a man." He couldn't decipher the mystery in her eyes. "Get yourself a man and learn to live and laugh." It was ridiculous to be speaking in this way, but for a hundred reasons she was to be pitied. With some surprise he believed he could picture the kind of life she must have had, and with a depth of feeling rare for him he thought how terrible it must be to grow up guileless and lonely and savage with it. She hadn't had a chance. "What will you want from a man?" he ventured.

Her mouth quivered. "Many things." She gave him the impression of staring into the past. And yet she answered him, almost confiding, as if a grille were between them. "What everyone wants, I suppose."

"What's that?" he prompted.

There was a rap at the door. Something intangible snapped and was gone. A sergeant bustled in and saluted.

"Beg pardon, sir, a message from the colonel to be prepared to evacuate headquarters at half-an-hour's notice."

"Where to?" The captain frowned, but didn't seem surprised.

"I'll have full details as soon as the orderly clerk's got them down."

"Very well."

"Another thing, sir."

"What?"

"The wounded prisoner, sir. He's been patched up. If you want to have him in I suggest now's as good a time as any."

Clodagh thought the captain would have her taken away when Sean was brought in. She'd heard it said that this was always how they worked—interrogating in isolation and trying to trap you with lies and so-called admissions by someone else. But she was wrong, at least in part. She stayed in the room and looked elsewhere when Sean limped through the door.

As he passed her by he muttered anxiously in Gaelic: "What does he know?"

She ignored him, obedient to herself. She turned her back. The searchlight had gone from the Green and troops were digging in around the bandstand. In the north-west corner she could see what remained of a chemist's shop— MacSweeney's, gilt lettering on a green fascia. The width of the Green away there was a pub—*The Saloon*. Spaced between them were the hotel and the house where the cellar was, and between these again were the ruins and the rubble past which she had crawled with Liam. . . . No harm could come of looking now.

Almost offhand the captain said to Sean: "You can sit if you wish."

The chair scraped as if it was shifted.

"Is it worth my while asking who you are?"

Silence.

"Obviously it isn't. So I'll start somewhere else. . . . When captured you were armed with a revolver. That's a fact, so you can quit stonewalling. A revolver, right? A revolver and ammunition which you got at Hafferty's."

"Who told you that?" The sullen voice. "Did she?"

"No, she didn't, but it's a fact, so let's move on." Time was short and he had so little to go on. "We aren't as much in the dark as you imagine." The captain tried a long shot.

"Peadar Ryan." Sean's mouth tightened and that was enough. "Peadar Ryan—wounded during a raid on a liquor store." The man was dead but he chose to unsettle Sean by pretending otherwise. "Ryan was at Hafferty's."

"News to me."

"And served in your squad."

"Never."

"He says he did."

"There's a hundred Ryans."

"Peadar."

"Alive?" Disbelief slowly moulded Sean's expression. "And he's supposed to have named names?"

"Some." Already the ice was thin.

"You'll need none from me, then."

"It's up to you." The captain raised his shoulders. "You can have it easy or you can have it hard. Ryan identified your squad—three men and a girl. Next you'll be telling me there's a hundred squads the same."

"The girl wasn't in our squad." Sean spoke in a tone of surly triumph. "She didn't belong with us."

"She was captured with you."

"We only got her last night. Peadar couldn't have known she existed." He didn't mind what he said now so long as he scored. "Try another bluff, captain." He turned and pointed across the Green. Smoke was writhing skywards, obscuring the sun. "We were holed up over there and we got the girl in exchange for some whiskey and canned meat. One of them she was with was sick, and this fellow came searching for what he could find. That's how we got her, and that's the truth. Peadar Ryan, my eye!"

Then he saw the captain's face.

"I didn't want her," he protested. "I didn't make the deal."

6

THE SERGEANT came back in. "Colonel's orders, sir." He placed a sheet of paper on the desk in front of the captain and went straight out again. Men were moving at the double in the street below. The captain didn't look at what was on the paper. For seconds on end he stared beyond Sean at Clodagh Lacey's back. An eighteen-pounder shook the windows and the sash-cords vibrated against the wood.

"Is what he says correct?" He delayed in vain, but he was accustomed to that. He said to her: "Were you with another squad?"

"I was."

"Holed up?"

"Holed up." She was gazing over the Green. Her voice was so low that he could scarcely hear her.

"Where?"

"I'm not telling."

"Who with?"

"I'm not telling."

He said mechanically: "We'll find out. You know we will. We always do in the end."

"Find out, then."

She turned his way and her eyes were glittering. Whenever he thought about her afterwards it was always her eyes he most vividly remembered: in that moment they were fierce and frightened beyond his understanding. And what she said was as unexpected as it was sudden.

"What will happen to me now?" Her hands were clenched, as if she were somehow clinging to an idea, a possibility.

"You'll be detained."

"Where?"

He was on the point of answering, but changed his mind. He pushed his private thoughts aside. He glanced down at the typewritten orders, then crossed to the door and opened it.

"Sergeant!"

"Sir?"

"What transport can you spare? These two are for the jail."

"Now, sir?"

"Right away."

"There's a lorry standing by, and we've got a car due back—"

"Use the lorry."

"Very good, sir."

"And then get these maps off the walls."

The sergeant stamped into the room as if powered by clockwork. "On your feet"—this to Sean. "And outside, the pair of you."

If he hadn't been there the captain might have said "Good luck" to Clodagh: almost certainly he would have done so. But in the event she didn't seem to notice him. She went past the desk as though he didn't exist. "Remember what I told you"—he might have said that too, had it been possible, had they been alone.

"Move along."

The landing was in chaos—kit-bags, bedding-rolls, boxes. The smell of yeast was as sour and clinging as ever. Men were clumping up and down the stairs. The sergeant went to the blanket-covered table and rummaged in the drawers until he found what he wanted. He dealt with Clodagh first, pulling her arms up from her sides so as to slap the handcuffs on her wrists. Sean cursed—"Christ above, what are we? Criminals?" But Clodagh made no protest.

The sergeant herded them to the top of the stairs. Sean led stiffly down and Clodagh followed. A voice called "What's the time, Nobby?" and another answered "Time we was bloody well out of here, if you ask me." She had no awareness of time. A truck was pulled in close to the exit. The cold was biting and the sky discoloured. The soldiers who'd filled the street in the dark of the night had gone, leaving only a makeshift brazier, choked with ash, to show for it. The sergeant detailed one of the sentries to ride in the truck and barked instructions at the driver. The truck was open, its canvas cladding rolled forward off the supporting stays and secured behind the driving-cab.

It was the kind of cold that in another country would have meant snow. Sean bared his teeth against it and struggled into the back of the truck. Clodagh went after him, shoved from behind. The sentry joined them and they all stood, clasping the stays. The tailboard was banged into position and the driver walked round to crank the engine.

"Twenty minutes," the sergeant said. "Just hand 'em over and get straight back."

The air was acrid with drifted gunsmoke. The truck U-turned on the cobbles and everybody lurched, hanging on. Clodagh held the central off-side stay, and the vibration coming through the double-handed grip spread like a numbness into the whole of her frame. The Green showed briefly as the driver took the corner, heading south, and she stared back at the buildings that had come between, watching the distance beginning to open up.

They went with a bone-shaking rattle across some tramlines. She knew what she was going to do, but their speed deterred her. The road was blurring beneath the wheels. They passed an intersection and she still couldn't steel herself. Two more went by before the driver braked and she found the nerve. Then she jumped. She did it without giving the slightest hint of what was in her mind, throwing herself over the side, momentarily heedless of the consequences, and her feet had touched before the escort realized what was happening.

Her legs seemed to snap at the knees. She flung up manacled hands to protect her head, then took the crashing impact, skidding, rolling like a body beached by a wave, somehow conscious of a series of shouts as she jolted to a standstill. For stunned moments she lay still, coiled into herself, hearing the truck squealing to a halt through a skull-splitting din all her own. Then she opened her eyes and scrambled upright, stupefied, blood flowing from a grazed cheek-bone, an excruciating pain in both ankles.

The escort fired before she had managed more than a

few yards, but he was well wide, fingers stiff with cold and dust floating into his face over the hard-braked truck. Clodagh crouched low, her brain clearing as she ran, every step deadening the pain. There was better cover on the other side of the street, but she had no choice—kiosk, scaffolding, pillar-box, overturned cart; these she used in a frenzy of desperation, weaving from side to side.

A second shot was closer. The ricochet sobbed overhead and she winced from it as she ran. Squares chalked for a game on a pavement, leaflets scattered in the gutters, a weathered crucifix on a wall. . . . She reached the corner she was making for and went panting into the comparative safety it offered—a narrow walk between one street and the next, stumpy posts at either end, a BICYCLING PROHIBITED sign. She ran on, the quick-thrown echoes clashing, hands together as if in supplication. She came out into the next street and went left and right, then right again, slowing now, lungs burning and the pain in her ankles renewed as the prospect of pursuit diminished.

God, oh God, oh God.

They had retreated past here, Kenny and Liam and herself. Three days ago, pulling back from the action by the picture-palace; the scars of the fighting were still to be seen. But now the tide was on the turn and troops were scattered between where she was and where she had to be.

Liam, she thought. Was he there still?

She went to ground behind a hoarding and waited until she'd recovered her breath. Deep inside she was pitilessly calm; the externals seemed to be happening to someone else.

Liam. And she had been ashamed.

Explosions blossomed in the pewter sky a fraction before the sound reached her. Gingerly she felt her ankles. At the self-same time, completely dissociated, she remembered her father and the pony and trap, clip-clop through the grey and white villages, and the cruel rains that sometimes came and killed the spring. "One day, girl, when things change for you. ..." She could feel her body hurting and nothing was very real, but she could also hear his voice and see the scene down all the years between the child she was then and whatever she was now.

The inner calmness remained, frozen into her heart. She squeezed out from behind the hoarding and limped away, raw-eyed from the pain. She was approaching the broken area of mean streets to the south-west of the Green. Patrols roamed at random, restless, mainly in section strength. They weren't on the look-out for an escaped stray, and she managed to avoid them. She worked in amongst a disorder of back-to-back houses and corner shops, everywhere destroyed and deserted as if a tornado had struck. Her breath steamed. Her jacket was ripped across the shoulders. In one place some men were looting; in another a horse lay stiff-legged dead and all the tram-wires had come down.

Mr. Halo.

Running a few yards, dodging this way and that, tears stinging the grazed cheek. Sometimes the firing stuttered from several directions at once, boomed, reverberated, tapped out a staccato drum-roll. She had drawn level with the southern end of the Green; to her right she glimpsed the trees. She was shot at from a rooftop and brickwork spat into her face from where the bullet struck. Later she was caught clambering a wall by a platoon hurriedly on the move and only their disbelief and hesitation saved her. She dropped and staggered clear and was spared.

Liam . . . Oh Christ, if he'd gone.

A sudden small-arms exchange made her crouch. Cross-fire. She was among the side streets into which they had watched the searchlight probing like an icy white bar. They, they. . . . But Liam was all; Kenny had diminished. She swerved from doorway to doorway, WARNING posters on a railing, glass and slates underfoot, spent shell-cases strewn in a tell-tale concentration. A rat broke cover with her. Repeatedly she went to ground, risked a short dash, retreated, found a new way, and there were moments in the fever of her mind when it seemed there had never been a time when anything was any different.

She came round to the end of the Green by way of the north-west corner, close to what remained of MacSweeney's. A burst of flame erupted in the nearest tree and the topmost branches blew to pieces. In all directions the air was patchy with smoke. An armoured car retreated with a roar within yards of where she lay, its machine-gun chattering, and for the first time in days—at an angle and indistinct—she thought she saw a scattering of men without uniforms.

She clenched her teeth and crossed in a scramble to the edge by MacSweeney's, hands locked, unbalanced as she ran. She had come this way before, nights ago, armed then, accepting orders. "Here," he'd yelled. "Over here." Now she crouched where she'd thrown herself and stared through the stinging smoke at where he'd led them into the shattered hotel.

Liam Gallagher.

And as if in obedience to the urgings of her will she suddenly heard him calling—"Clodagh! . . . Clodagh!"—and knew with a kind of singing numbness that she hadn't wished and struggled in vain.

She went up the side of the cone of rubble to where the bathroom opening was and tumbled in, pain forgotten, weakness forgotten, finding a last reserve of strength.

"Clodagh . . . Jesus, girl."

She couldn't speak.

"Where in God's name've you sprung from?"

She turned sideways from him, gulping air, on her knees, and he saw the handcuffs for the first time.

"When—?" He grabbed hold of her. "And your cheek...."

He didn't seem to know where to start or how to finish. "What's happened to you?"

"I . . . jumped."

"From what?"

"A lorry."

He had her by the wrists. "How long have those been there?"

"Long enough." She had never known him without his cap.

The sky flashed and the ruin shook; dust cascaded down. But they seemed oblivious of it. There was only themselves, alive still, survived, the two of them.

He said: "Kenny's dead, Clodagh."

His cap covered Kenny's face and Kenny was stretched out on his back beside the bath.

"He's gone, God rest him." Liam lifted the cap to let her see: like marble. "He gave it up towards dawn. It was hopeless."

Her eyes had lost their transparency and she didn't utter, just looked and went on looking, impassive, as if every scrap of emotion had been drained and she had no feelings left. What passed in her mind he could only guess.

"Where did they get you? When they made the search?"

She didn't answer.

"I heard them," he said. "But they never came this far along. Is that when they—?"

"We broke out." He might have been a stranger, never there, not knowing what the place was like. Not involved.

"We had a back way."

"All of you got clear?"

"All of us."

Her gaze was on the move, here, there, blank and impassive—the chamber-pot on the banister-rail, the Infant of Prague statuette upended in the fireplace.

"And then?" Liam said.

"Then we got taken."

"All of you?"

"Two of us."

Her voice was toneless and her eyes were vacant, dead at the centre. "Which two?" he wanted to ask, but did not; could not. "What became of the other one?" But could not. One day, maybe. But not now. Wasn't it enough for now that she was with him again, and triumph on its way?

"Question you, did they?"

"That's right."

"What did they want?"

"Names, mostly." Plaster in the bath, the tap dripping. She saw and heard. "Names, places, squads. . . . We were down at the other end, above the baker's shop."

"What made them put you in the lorry?"

"They're after pulling out, that's why."

"Did both of you jump?"

She shook her head. "Only me."

"How did you know I'd still be here?"

"I didn't. But I wanted it so."

He smiled—a worn shy smile with his teeth covered. His stubble was thick and dark now. Kenny's rifle near his body, an empty corned beef tin, an inch of whiskey in a bottle. . . . She looked at them.

Two crunching detonations sounded near the Green. Liam crawled to the parapet and peered over, not using the mirror.

Clodagh said to him: "Give me Kenny's gun."

"You'll never manage it with those things on you."

"I will so," she said.

He picked up the rifle and held it towards her. She separated her wrists as far as they could go and took hold of the rifle, the fingers of her left hand splayed beneath the magazine, her right hand tight around the trigger-guard, thumb straining for the safety-catch.

Liam watched the muzzle waver. "It's no good," he said. "You'll be no good like that."

"I will," she said, and shot him through the heart.

His body jerked with the same convulsive finality as her father's. In a kind of delirium she noticed this one fact. Then she mounted the slope of rubble and stood on the crest of the parapet.

The smoke had cleared. The machine-gunner by the bandstand opened up as soon as he saw her. The rubble shrieked and exploded all around. Instinctively she tried to shift the bolt, but could not, not with her hands the way they were. And it didn't matter. She staggered forward, only seconds remaining. Yet while they lasted and she struggled to reload, her mind was concerned with a rushing tide of things which had been with her since childhood—about growing up and being chosen and loving and being loved, about trust and respect and growing older and making a reality of the lonely dream. All these.

"Next time," the gunner said to his number two. "What d'you bet?"